Praise for

DARK PASSAGES:
Tristan & Karen
Book Four in The Brethren Series™

"An amazing read! With a hero like this, the bite—and everything that comes with it—is well worth the blood!" — *NY Times* and *USA Today* best-selling author Sharon Sala

5 Stars: "Be prepared for heartache, rich drama, and a lot of blood lust!" — LoveRomancePassion.com

"My favorite of all the [Brethren Series] books. I loved Tristan—he is strong, powerful, stubborn and very alpha male, just like I like them!" — Paranormal Haven

DARK PASSAGES: Tristan & Karen
Book Four in The Brethren Series™
by Sara Reinke

Edited by Jennifer Barker
Published by Bloodhorse Press, LLC
www.bloodhorsepress.com

Cover artwork by Kimberly Killion, Hot Damn Designs!
www.hotdamndesigns.com

DEDICATION

To my readers, whose support, encouragement and friendship have made this book possible.

CHAPTER ONE

Tristan Morin shoved Karen Pierce back into the nearest wall and pressed his mouth against hers. The warmth of her lips, the sweetness of her tongue, saliva, and breath—it was enough to strip the senses from him.

"Tell me to stop," he whispered, because it was all he could do not to wrench her head back by the hair and sink his teeth into the hot, pulsating length of her carotid artery. His canines had extended, dropping from recessed grooves in his gumline. His pupils had enlarged, an ancient, primitive reflex that left them dilating wide enough to nearly swallow the visible portions of his irises and corneas. In this sudden, extremely light-sensitive field of vision, Karen's pale skin seemed to glow, miniscule droplets of perspiration glistening against her face like diamonds.

"No." She shook her head defiantly, her cheeks flushed, her blonde hair askew, her blue eyes glossy and round with eager anticipation.

He reached between them, ripping open her blouse with a single forceful yank. Buttons popped loose, scattering against the floor; she wore no bra beneath. He drew back long enough to shrug his way out of his own shirt, then pushed himself into her, feeling the incredible heat of her body, the bullet points of her nipples against his chest.

"Tell me to stop," he pleaded again, because if he didn't, he was going to feed from her. *And I can't do that. God help me, I can't.*

Karen locked eyes with him. "No."

Her fingers tangled in his hair as he slid his hands down her torso, following the slim indentation of her waist, the outward swells of her hips. She'd worn a black skirt to the funeral, something simple, with a hem that fell to midthigh. He pulled it up now toward her navel, then opened the fly of his pants. Seizing one side of her panties, he gave a jerk, ripping them away from her, then caught her buttocks in his hands and hoisted her off the ground.

Her legs wrapped around his midriff, her hands splayed across his shoulder blades, and when he entered into her, filling her in a single, swift stroke, she stiffened, her breath catching sharply.

Crushing her back into the wall, he drove himself into her, feeling her fingernails hook into his back. Almost immediately, she came, as if their rough, harried foreplay had brought her to the breaking point and he'd just driven her over the edge. The sudden rush of blood through her body, adrenaline-infused and endorphin-laced, was almost more than he could bear.

His bedroom was upstairs, a loft overlooking the open floor plan of his A-frame home. With a soft grunt, he pulled her near, carrying her toward the stairs, her legs still viselike around his waist. This left her throat vulnerably exposed and close to his mouth, his fangs. He was salivating, his mouth flooded, his jaw aching. She knew what he wanted and wasn't afraid, not of him or his sudden overwhelming urge to feed, and somehow this realization excited him even more.

Please don't let me do this, he thought as he reached the top of the stairs, carrying her toward his bed. Her shoes fell off along the way, black leather pumps that tumbled noisily to the floor and that he kicked out of his path. He opened his mouth, letting the tips of his fangs press against her, lightly at first, then dimpling her skin, sinking slowly, deliberately. *Oh, God, please don't let me bite her!*

With a hoarse cry, he pushed Karen away, and she fell back against the mattress, her eyes wide with startled surprise. Without giving her time to recover—or for him to reconsider the aborted bite attempt—Tristan flipped her onto her stomach, clasped her hips, and pulled her back against the bedspread, spearing into her from behind.

As he fell into another powerful rhythm, he held her hands against the mattress, his fingers laced through hers, and she arched her back, leaning into his shoulder, grinding her buttocks into him. He came hard, release crashing over him in shuddering waves, and as it did, that relentless urge to feed, to bury his teeth into the soft, sweet meat of her throat, was mercifully obliterated.

Because I don't think I could've held out much longer, he thought, crumpling onto the bed beside her, letting his breath escape in a long, heavy sigh. *And if I give into the bloodlust...if I feed from Karen...then, oh, Christ, I'm screwed. Royally.*

****

Karen rolled onto her side, spooning against Tristan. His eyes were closed, his face glossed with sweat, his hair swept messily across his brow. She could see his canine teeth beginning to recede, slipping back beneath the cover of his upper lip and into his gums.

This has to be a dream.

With a smile, she draped her hand lightly against his chest. Like hers, his skin was flushed, infused with heat, sweat-soaked from exertion, and beneath her fingertips, she could feel the rapid-fire rhythm of his heartbeat.

Tristan and his family were of a race of beings who collectively referred to themselves as the Brethren. By any other definition, they were vampires—long-lived carnivores who seemed to never age or tire, whose canine teeth could elongate at will so that they could feed. Unlike the cheesy horror-movie variety or sparkling, ethereal creatures from

7

teen-age melodramas, the Brethren lived seamlessly among
humans, not preying upon them. Or at least, the Morin
family, including Tristan, didn't.

Their home was a communal estate along the
mountainous shores of Emerald Bay, off Lake Tahoe in
California. More than sixty members of the Morin clan lived
in dozens of houses scattered among the pine trees and
aspens. For much of the year, many of the houses went
unoccupied, with Morin cousins, brothers, sisters, and
assorted kin out and about in the human world, living
undetected, going about otherwise unextraordinary, even
mundane, lives. Tristan lived on the lakefront property, as
did Karen. She was the sole human allowed access to, and
intimate knowledge of, the Morins' carefully guarded world.
In addition to homesteads, the property also housed a one-
of-a-kind medical clinic that specialized in the treatment of
Brethren, who with their unique physiologies and biological
needs required equally individualized treatments. She'd
been hired to work at the clinic by Tristan's grandfather,
Michel. The benefits included free on-site room and board, a
house of her own, and a view of the lake below.

Another perk of the job was working with Tristan, being
near him, day in and day out.

He wanted this. He wanted me.

The first time she'd laid eyes on him was at the Sierra
Nevada Medical Center in Reno five years earlier. She was an

oncology-certified nurse and he was one of a handful of
residents on rotation in the ward. His youthful appearance
had belied an astonishing clinical proficiency beyond his
years, but more than this—there was something about him
that she'd felt drawn toward, as if he was somehow
magnetically charged, exerting some unseen, unbidden pull
on her mind and heart. She'd never told him this, of
course—or anyone else, for that matter—and had sure as hell
never acted on it.

Until now.

Tristan's mother had been buried yesterday, a small
service at a family plot less than a ten-minute walk from
where Karen now stood. Lisette Morin had been sick for a
long time, languishing in a unresponsive state of persistent
catatonia, her mind virtually stripped in the aftermath of a
violent hemorrhagic stroke years earlier. Her death had been
inevitable, a fact that had never been lost upon her physician
son, who had tended faithfully to her care. Still, however
expected, the loss had left Tristan grief stricken. He'd stood
at the graveside, eyes fixed on the glossy casket draped in an
arrangement of lilies and roses, listening as his grandfather,
Michel, had offered a quiet sermon meant to comfort, but to
which Tristan had seemed oblivious.

After the service, as the gathering of Morin friends and
family had broken apart, she'd felt a momentary bewildered

thrill as he reached for her, catching her by the hand, pulling her near.

"My house," he'd whispered, his lips brushing her ear as he spoke with intimate proximity, a gravelly hoarseness to his voice. "Now."

He'd said no more but hadn't needed to. She'd seen it in his eyes, what he meant with those words. She'd followed him down the rutted path back to his home as he held her hand lightly but firmly in his own. It had seemed so surreal to her, and she trembled all the while with a mixture of anxiety and anticipation. Despite her association with vampires on a daily basis, she'd never once been bitten by any of them.

Long before Tristan was even born, Michel had come up with revolutionary ideas about Brethren nature and behavior that had flown in the face of what others of their kind had believed for millennia. His first such controversial hypothesis had been that Brethren weren't meant to feed from humans at all, but rather, from *each other*, a physiological preference supported by the Brethren's innate ability to heal quickly and fully from almost any injury, and the fact that heightened psychokinetic abilities only developed in those Brethren who fed regularly on their fellows. This particular supposition had led to the Morin clan being forced into exile, segregated from other Brethren clans centuries earlier.

Karen had been told that the bloodlust—the instinctive need the Brethren felt to feed—was strongly akin to sexual desire, so much so that when a Brethren male was aroused before lovemaking, his canine teeth would extend, his pupils dilating so his eyes would seemingly turn black. Last night, it had happened to Tristan, but rather than shocking or frightening her, his appearance had only turned Karen on all the more.

Tell me to stop, he'd whispered to her, and she remained uncertain as to whether he'd meant making love to her or trying to feed from her. She'd told him no each time, not caring which.

Still smiling, she closed her eyes, feeling the warmth of his chest against her cheek, breathing in the lingering hint of his cologne. Now she could hear the pounding measure of his heartbeat as it slowed inexorably to a less frantic pace.

I love you, Tristan, she thought with a contented sigh.

****

I love you, Tristan.

Tristan wished he could block her thoughts out of his mind. But like his body, it had been unhinged by the bloodlust, and there would be no reining it in, no containing or controlling the powerful telepathy he normally commanded with accustomed and comfortable ease.

Even the simple act of her touching his chest was enough to make him tremble, as if a current of electricity stole through her body and into his own. He was too exhausted to pull away from her, however, even though he knew it would be safest.

Because if I don't, the bloodlust might return, he thought, gritting his teeth, forcing himself to roll over, turn his back on Karen. *I can't take that chance.*

He could pick her out of a crowded room; with his eyes closed and his hands tied behind his back, he was invariably, unerringly drawn to Karen. Her scent—the intermingling fragrances of her skin, hair, breath, and blood—left him dizzy, nearly drunk with desire if he stood too close to her for too long. He'd never reacted to a human like that, and had fought the temptation to yield to that incessant need every day from the moment they'd met.

Which is why Michel brought her here, Tristan thought with a frown. *And why I can't give in to her. It's exactly what the son of a bitch wants.*

****

The next morning, Karen woke to the sweet strains of piano music. Her eyes opened a bleary half-mast, and she blinked sleepily across the breadth of a king-sized bed draped in white sheets and a pale, pillowy down comforter.

Tristan's bed, she thought with a soft smile, even though there was no sign of Tristan. The music continued from downstairs, unabated and intricate, giving her a pretty good idea of where she'd find him.

It was real, then. The thought made her smile shyly, her hand darting to her mouth. *It really happened. Tristan made love to me.*

Her smile still tugged at the corners of her mouth as she slipped out of bed. She was naked except for the skirt she'd worn the day before. This was tangled around her waist, the hem hiked so high, it hugged her more like a belt or bandeau, and she tried to tug it back down toward her knees. Her high-heeled shoes lay in a pile by the closet door, and as she slipped them back on, she spied a rumpled T-shirt on top of his nearby dresser. She slipped it over her head, then glanced at herself in a nearby mirror—wrinkled clothes, sleep-tousled hair—and winced.

God, I look rough, she thought, trying to smooth her hair down, tucking it behind her ears. *But it was worth it. Every last glorious minute.*

As Karen crept down the stairs, she could look out across the open interior of the first floor below. Tristan's house was framed by towering windows on all sides, awarding a nearly panoramic view of the surrounding vista overlooking Lake Tahoe's Emerald Bay. Some of these opened onto a large adjoining patio and had been left deliberately ajar to allow the crisp, cool morning air to filter inside.

She saw Tristan seated at a grand piano, dressed only in a pair of sweatpants, his chest and arms bare. Although he faced the keyboard, his hands rested at his sides, his fingers hooked over the edge of the bench beneath him as if he braced himself against an impact or a blow. His head was tilted slightly backward, his eyes closed, a soft cleft between his brows suggesting deep concentration. In front of him, she could see the keys moving up and down, flying in rapid-fire procession, as if invisible hands drilled against them.

Which, in a manner of speaking, was exactly what was happening.

Because he fed from other Brethren, Tristan was endowed with telekinesis. Blessed with a natural ear for music, he could use this unnatural and, in Karen's opinion, extraordinary ability to hear any piece of music, then play it for himself, all without laying a finger on a piano. He could play by hand, of course, having been taught in his youth by his now deceased mother. However, he did so rarely, preferring instead to play by benefit of his mind. The *Brethren way,* as he called it.

The music abruptly faltered, and he lowered his head, opening his eyes as he glanced over his shoulder at her. She hadn't made a sound, had been trying her best, in fact, to be as quiet as possible lest she disturb him, but she may as well have not bothered. The Brethren were also telepaths.

He probably sensed me the minute I woke up.

"I'm sorry," she said. "I didn't mean to..."

He shook his head, cutting her off. "It's all right."

"The music was beautiful," she said. "What was it?"

"Ravel. *Gaspard de la nuit.*" He leaned back, resting his elbows against the piano keys with a disharmonic sound. "Listen, I'm glad you're up."

"Why?" she asked, a mischievous smile tugging the corners of her lips. She considered going over to him, straddling him on the piano bench, hiking her skirt back up to her hips to allow him easy access.

"I've got some things to do before I have to check in at the clinic today," he said, stopping her cold in her tracks. "I need to take off in a few minutes."

"What?" Karen blinked at him, bewildered. She didn't know what she'd been expecting—if not an encore performance of the previous evening's main event, then at least maybe a cup of coffee and a smile—but this sure wasn't it.

"I can give you a ride back up the hill to your place, if you want," he offered.

What is he talking about? He can't be serious. She stared at him, wounded. *Not after last night.*

Although the Morins didn't feed from humans, they *did* intermarry with them, have sexual relations, even children with them. Not Tristan, however. While many of his siblings, cousins, and kin were the results of these human-Brethren matings, Tristan had been born to a Brethren mother, sired by a Brethren father. He was the last full-blooded Brethren to be born among the Morins. Because of that distinction, he wanted to breed with a Brethren woman to continue his bloodline.

Not a human, she thought, her eyes stinging with tears, because that was part of the reason she'd been so excited by the urgency she'd seen in his eyes as they'd left the gravesite. *I thought he wanted me.*

Less than a week earlier, he'd damn near married a young Brethren woman named Tessa Noble, not because he'd loved her—he'd hardly even known her—but because it would have meant, in his estimation at least, a suitable breeding partner.

Although she'd never admit it aloud, she'd been deeply hurt when she learned of the aborted elopement—so much so, she'd nearly quit the clinic. She'd typed up her letter of resignation in her fit of wounded outrage. Only her father's voice inside her mind had stopped her from turning it in, a patient cadence and gentle words she remembered fondly from her youth:

"Your mother and I, we didn't raise any quitters, Kay."

Although her father was in Manhattan, Kansas—three states and two time zones away—he'd still been able to impart wisdom upon her. In the end, Karen had shoved the letter in the glove compartment and forgotten about it—until now.

"So do you want a ride?" Tristan asked again.

Forcing herself to smile despite bright patches of hot, humiliated color blazing in her cheeks, she said, "That's okay. I...I can walk."

He cocked his head. "You sure?"

"Yeah. It's not far."

"But..." It was his turn to look uncertain. "It's cold."

"I don't mind." All at once, Karen wanted to get the hell out of there, because she'd been through this before—the big brush-off—with ex-boyfriends galore. She'd come to expect it from just about every man she felt attracted to anymore.

But not you, Tristan, she thought, pressing her lips together in a strained line. *God, I never would have expected it from you. Not in a million years.*

"Let me at least get you a coat, then." When he stood, his expression looked sheepish. He could read her thoughts if he wanted, and though she had no way of knowing whether his mind was open to her, he wasn't blind or deaf. He saw the tears in her eyes, heard the damnable warble in her voice.

"No, thanks." She bee-lined for the door, T-shirt, miniskirt, and bare legs be damned. But he could move impossibly fast when he wanted to, another Brethren benefit, and with a sudden blur out of the corner of her eye, he beat her to it, blocking her path.

"Karen." In that moment, he looked for all the world like a lost little boy, vulnerable, wounded to the core. His mouth opened slightly, as if he meant to speak, but then catching himself and thinking better of it, he pressed his lips together. She'd lost him again.

Not that I'd ever had him, she thought sadly. That much was painfully obvious.

"Here," he said at length, reaching for a coat rack just beyond the front door. His parka hung here, black and down-filled, and he slipped it from the hook. For a moment, he leaned toward her, close enough for her to feel the warmth radiating from his skin as he drew the coat around her shoulders. "There's frost outside."

Didn't last night mean anything to you, Tristan? she thought helplessly, swatting at a tear as it rolled down her cheek before he might notice. *Don't I?*

Abruptly he drew back, not just leaning away, but backpedaling as if he'd smelled something offensive or she'd slapped him in the face. The gesture hurt her more than any words or physical blows ever could have, and with a frown, she shoved the coat off, letting it fall heavily to the floor.

"Keep it. I'll be fine," she assured him drily. Hoping he was listening, that he could hear the venom in her thoughts, she added: *It's the frost in here that's getting to me, anyway.*

CHAPTER TWO

Smooth, Tristan told himself after Karen had left, slamming the front door behind her. From the other side, as she'd hurried away, he could have sworn he'd heard her utter a soft, shuddering sob. *She's crying. Terrific. And the Asshole of the Year award now officially belongs to me.*

He forked his fingers through his hair, not missing the fact that his hand was shaking. Even that momentary closeness to her as he'd put his coat around her shoulders had been enough to stir the bloodlust in him.

God, she smells good, he'd thought, closing his eyes and allowing himself a luxurious split second to breathe her scent in deeply. It had been all he could do not to draw her into his arms, to nuzzle beneath the warm shelf of her chin and let his hands fall against the soft swells of her breasts. In an instant, he'd wanted her, had been ready to take her again, this time right there on the floor of his entryway; to feel her long legs twine around him again, to listen to her soft, breathless sounds of pleasure as she moved beneath him. He'd wanted her so badly—body and blood—that he'd physically recoiled from her, forcing himself to move, to stumble backward, lest he lose control again.

As he picked his parka off the floor and returned it to the hook by the door, he noticed he could still discern her in the air. Leaning forward, he sniffed the coat experimentally, but it hadn't been against her body long enough to capture her fragrance.

Then where is that coming from? Puzzled, he glanced around and caught sight of something white in a rumpled pile on the floor by his sofa. Karen's blouse.

Goddamn it, Tristan thought with a scowl as he tromped over to retrieve it. He snatched it, then held it out away from him, like it was a dead rat he'd discovered in his pantry. *I can't keep this in my house, not even in the trash outside. I'll go crazy from her scent.*

While one side of his house was flanked with windows, against another, a broad creek-stone fireplace had been constructed. He had at least a half cord of firewood stacked outside, which he'd cut himself and left to season some six months earlier.

I'll burn it, he thought, balling the blouse in his hands and marching toward the fireplace. But just as he reached the hearth, he paused, looking down at the wadded tangle of white silk.

God, I never would have expected it from you, he'd heard Karen think as he'd broken her heart. *Not in a million years.*

You don't understand, he thought, wishing he could explain to her, make things right for her somehow. *I can't be with you again, Karen. I shouldn't have been with you last night, but I lost my head...lost my senses. That's what happens when I'm around you too long with nothing like work to distract me.*

He drew the tattered remains of Karen's blouse momentarily to his face, closed his eyes, and remembered the warmth of her skin, the salty sweetness of her kiss, the intoxicating musk of her blood.

Why did I do that? Why did I have to go and sleep with her? he thought, even though he knew the answer. Ever since his mother's death, he'd felt grief-stricken and alone, as if someplace vital inside of him had been scraped empty and raw. He'd been vulnerable, lonely, in need of comfort, companionship. In need of Karen.

I still need her, he realized, then frowned. With an angry cry, he threw the shirt into the fireplace, then turned and headed for the door. He was bare chested and barefoot, and the frost-crusted grass crunched beneath the soles of his feet. In an instant, his breath frosted in the air, framing his face in a dim halo, and he strode around the corner, heading for the woodpile in his back yard.

****

Karen's house was less than 200 yards from Tristan's, but along a zigzagging path cut by the gravel road, or more directly if she went through the dense pine woods between them. On some winter mornings, she could see the hint of smoke from his chimney, or the glint of sunlight off his windshield or truck mirrors as he'd pull in or out of his driveway.

One of her shoe heels broke en route, the spindly columns ill equipped for cross-country trekking. She fell as her footing gave way, skinning her palms and knees, and then limped and hobbled the rest of the miserable way, cursing Tristan under her breath all the while.

Once home, she kicked off her ruined shoes and crammed them both unceremoniously into the kitchen trash. Then, because she could still smell his damned cologne in his T-shirt, she yanked it off and threw it into her fireplace.

I'm not going to cry again, she told herself firmly as she squatted in front of the hearth. *I'm not going to cry, goddamn it. I'm not going to cry over him anymore.*

She'd been no more than a half step out his door before bursting into tears, hating herself for it but helpless to prevent it. Pressing her lips together to muffle the sound, she'd staggered, nearly blinded by tears, down the steps of his front stoop. It had been cold out, and she'd spent the duration of her hike home miserable, hiccupping and shivering.

In a small metal bin beside the hearth, she kept a ready stock of firewood. She'd split it herself only a few weeks earlier, wearing blisters into the pads of her palms from gripping the ax handle so fiercely. Tristan had noticed, asked about them, then laughed when she'd explained.

"Why didn't you just ask me to do it?" he'd asked, the unspoken implication being that as a woman, she was utterly incapable of tending to something like chopping firewood on her own. She'd considered telling him that she'd once split firewood on a regular basis on her father's cattle farm growing up—along with driving a tractor, pitching hay, shoveling cow shit, and tending to dozens of other chores he'd undoubtedly consider *man's work*.

"He's an asshole," she muttered, tossing wood into the fireplace, pinning the T-shirt beneath. She struck a match and used it for kindling, watching the white cotton first smolder, then spark, then at length begin to burn.

Good riddance, she thought, and because the chill in the air had caused goose bumps to rise, she stood up, wrapping her arms around herself as she went to the bathroom. Here, she ran the hot tap in her cedar-lined shower until the narrow room was filled with thick steam.

She stepped beneath the nozzle and drew the curtain shut behind her, closing her eyes as the stinging spray immediately pelted the top of her head. She began to wash, rubbing soap into a sudsy lather between her hands and then grinding it into her skin with a ferocious sort of determination.

I want to wash it away—everything that happened last night. Every place he touched me, kissed me.

Tilting her head back, she opened her mouth wide and let the shower flood her cheeks. She spit, then repeated, because she could remember the flavor of his mouth, the heat of his breath, the urgent insistence—the unrestrained desire—she'd felt in his kiss. With her eyes closed, she could remember the way he sounded, his voice, ragged with need: *"Tell me to stop."* When he'd come inside her, he'd uttered a low, breathless cry, his entire body going rigid behind her, his fingers clamping fiercely, reflexively against her own.

It had been the best sex of her entire life. Just like she'd always imagined it would be with him.

Damn you, Tristan.

****

Tristan had lied to Karen. He didn't have a damn thing going on that morning, except for being due to work at the clinic by noon. By the time he arrived, his first—and likely only—patient of the day was waiting for him: Brandon Noble.

Like Tristan, Brandon was full-blooded Brethren. He'd recently suffered serious burns on his face and torso, but thanks to his birthright and the accelerated healing abilities that came with it, he'd recovered quickly, with no scars to show for the suffering. At least, none that were visible.

"I hate to tell you this." He made sure to look the younger man directly in the eye when speaking. Although telepathic like Tristan, Brandon was deaf and mute. When not spoken to directly through his mind, he could read lips. After a long moment spent looking solemnly at Brandon, Tristan smiled. "But you're going to be just fine."

For no other reason than he hated the idea of wrapping up so soon, and being otherwise alone for the rest of the afternoon, Tristan had put Brandon through his medical paces, practicing all the standard routines and then some—eye exam, ears, EKG, CBC, anything he could think of to kill some time and occupy his attention, keep his mind off of Karen.

Brandon had looked worried until Tristan smiled; then he laughed soundlessly. *Thanks to you,* he said telepathically. He started buttoning his shirt as Tristan turned to make a quick note in his medical chart, then asked hesitantly, *Would you be able to write me a prescription?*

Puzzled, Tristan glanced over his shoulder. *You should be okay. That Z-Pak I put you on prophylactically keeps working for five days past the last dose.*

No. Brandon shook his head, then cut his eyes away. *It's just, we're leaving today.* When Tristan raised a curious brow, he elaborated. *Me and Lina. We're flying down to Miami, then renting a car, visiting her mom for a while, at least six weeks. She's been really sick...*

Tristan nodded, interjecting. *Breast cancer. Lina told me.*

Brandon looked momentarily toward the examination room door, beyond which Lina Jones, his human girlfriend, sat waiting for him. *I know Lina's been really worried about her.*

Because his own mother's funeral had been only the day before, Tristan managed a pained smile. *I can imagine.*

Brandon blinked at Tristan and, to judge by his suddenly sheepish expression, realized his faux pas. *I'm sorry, I didn't...,* he began.

Tristan shook his head. *It's all right.*

Anyway, it's just... With a sigh, Brandon raked his fingers through the crown of his hair, then hopped down from the examination table. *Back in Kentucky, I was taking these pills. My friend Jackson got them for me in his name, had them shipped to the great house. I'm not really planning to head back that way anytime soon.*

Tristan leaned back against the counter, his curiosity piqued. "What kind of pills?" he asked aloud, which made Brandon cut his eyes uneasily again toward the waiting room.

Wellbutrin, Brandon said.

Are you a smoker? Tristan asked, and Brandon shook his head, visibly puzzled.

Wellbutrin's an antidepressant, Tristan explained. *It's frequently prescribed to help people quit smoking, to ease the withdrawal symptoms.*

With an *aha!* sort of expression, Brandon nodded. *Oh,* he said. *But that's not why I need it.* Still looking somewhat uneasy, he hesitated for a long moment before continuing. *See, last year, I read an article in this magazine about how certain kinds of medicines can cause different side effects. It talked about antidepressants, about how they sometimes cause...*

His voice inside Tristan's mind faltered. Bewildered, Tristan tried to fill in the blank. *Constipation?* he asked. *Dry mouth? Headache? Wellbutrin blocks the action of acetylcholine, causing what's called anticholinergic effects...*

Brandon shook his head. *Not those.* He looked at Tristan, embarrassed, nearly pleading. *Sexual side effects. They can inhibit your sex drive.*

Surprised because this was not the answer he was expecting from an otherwise sound and physically normal twenty-one-year-old male—and one with a damn fine-looking girlfriend, at that—Tristan blinked. "What?" he asked, forgetting himself and speaking aloud.

I don't want that to happen to me, Brandon said quickly, his eyes flown wide, holding out his hands. *That doesn't happen, not normally. I mean, it hasn't so far, at least not while me and Lina, we've been...* Blushing brightly, flustered

27

again, he shoved his fingers through his hair. *Look, it helps control the bloodlust, okay? I started taking it because I figured if it could affect one kind of lust, then why not the other?*

Tristan raised his brow, surprised anew. *And it worked?*

Brandon nodded. *For the most part. I was able to keep it under control, anyway. Back in Kentucky, I didn't want to go through the bloodletting, feed from humans, so I needed to be able to keep the bloodlust in check.*

But you don't need to anymore, Tristan told him kindly. *You're with friends now—safe here, Brandon. I keep trying to tell you that. You can feed from any of us whenever you need to.*

But I'm getting ready to leave, Brandon said for the second time in the course of their conversation, and now, all at once, it made sense to Tristan. *I'm not going to be around you, not for a while, at least for a month. I'll be in Florida with Lina and her family. Around humans, Tristan.*

"I see your point," Tristan remarked thoughtfully.

That Brandon was terrified of losing control while away from the sanctuary of his fellow Brethren was apparent; even if Tristan hadn't been able to read his mind, he could see it plainly in his face. And the truth of the matter was, Tristan could sympathize with him completely.

Because I've been trying to fight off the bloodlust myself over the past twelve hours.

So would you mind helping me out? Brandon asked. *Writing me a prescription?*

With a smile, Tristan clapped him affably on the shoulder. "I'll do you one better, Brandon," he said, seeing the perfect opportunity to get away from not only the doldrums afternoon that surely lay in store, but from Karen too. *Because I can't face her again, not today, not after last night.* "I'll go get the pills for you myself."

****

"You shouldn't leave your door unlocked."

With a startled cry, Karen whirled as she stepped out of the bathroom. Steam still wafted out of the ajar door in her wake, and she'd been holding a towel wrapped around her torso with one hand, swatting her wet hair with another when the sound of a woman's voice from the living room had stopped her in her tracks.

"Naima," she gasped, managing a shaky laugh when she realized her company.

Naima Morin was Tristan's half sister, although she was older than him by more than 175 years. Her mother had been a human slave in the Morin family household during the Civil War era, shortly after the Brethren clans had first migrated from their ancestral homes in France. It was Karen's understanding, to hear tell of things from Michel, that Naima's mother had been a woman of extraordinary beauty. She found this easy to believe, considering Naima had seemed to inherit this remarkable turn of fortune.

Catlike and elegant, Naima's lean, athletic frame was tautly muscled, without a hint of fat or softness. Her skin was the color of milk chocolate, her eyes a shade or two darker, her hair kept short-cropped and close to the contours of her head. She had the kind of aristocratic facial features any super model would envy.

"You scared me half to death," Karen told her, readjusting her grasp on the front of her towel before inadvertently flashing the other woman.

"I didn't mean to." Naima smiled as she lounged on Karen's couch, her long legs extended, her ankles crossed. This comfortable position belied a peculiar strain in her face, however, a sort of visible uneasiness that was uncharacteristic for her and for which Karen had no accounting.

"The door was unlocked. I let myself in." Naima first uncrossed her legs, then swung them around, rising gracefully from the sofa. "You should lock it from now on. For a little while, anyway."

Puzzled, Karen frowned. "Why?"

The Morin family compound was well hidden and fully secured, accessible through security-gated entrances. It was out of the way, even for tourists who flocked in droves to see the beaches of Emerald Bay below them, or the neighboring

historic Vikingsholm mansion. Even though most of the
Morin houses were vacant the majority of the year, as a rule,
they remained unlocked because no one in the family
mistrusted another enough to guard their belongings so
closely or carefully. Karen had always liked this relaxed,
carefree sort of lifestyle; it had reminded her of her
childhood, the simple securities she and her family had
enjoyed in her Kansas hometown.

"I don't want to upset you," Naima began as she walked
toward Karen.

Trust me, Karen thought about saying. *Nothing can
upset me more than your brother has today.*

"Last night, Michel and I ran into someone out in the
woods," Naima said. "His name was Jean Luc Davenant.
He's like us, one of the Brethren."

"Davenant?" Karen frowned thoughtfully for a moment,
struggling to place the familiar-sounding name. "You mean,
one of the family who tried to kill Augustus and Brandon
back in Kentucky? Brandon's sister, Tessa, is married to one
of them, isn't she?"

"*Was* married," Naima corrected, because Martin
Davenant, Tessa's abusive husband, was dead. Augustus
Noble had killed him. "Jean Luc is his uncle."

"What was he doing here?"

"I don't know." Naima shook her head. "But Michel told
me he'd sensed him in the forest, snooping around. It makes

sense that one or more of them might have tracked Augustus and Brandon back here, back to us, when they left Kentucky."

Karen remembered another reason the name *Davenant* was known to her. "They're the ones who tried to murder your family, aren't they?" she asked, and Naima nodded.

"In 1815, they burned our great house to the ground, yes. Their objective was to kill everyone inside."

But you'd already escaped, Karen thought. *Augustus Noble found out what the Davenants had planned, and he warned Michel, helped the family to escape. The Davenants didn't know, didn't realize it, not at first, anyway.*

"Probably not until last night," Naima agreed, because unlike most other Brethren, she kept her mind wide open nearly all the time, making her privy to the thoughts of just about anyone within her immediate vicinity.

"Jean Luc Davenant attacked us," she continued. "He doesn't possess the telekinesis of one who has fed from another Brethren, but he's still physically very powerful. We fended him off, drove him away, but Michel thinks he'll be back. And that he won't be alone this time."

"What will they do?" Karen asked. "The Davenants, I mean. When they find out the Morins are still alive?"

Allistair Davenant was the worst among them, right? she thought. *He was their Elder, the one who hated Augustus.*

"I imagine they'll try to kill us again," Naima replied grimly. "They hated Michel too, just as much as—if not more than—Augustus. And Allistair was far from the worst. There were seven Davenant brothers, each just as dangerous—and as deadly—as the last."

She walked toward the front door to let herself out, her posture pristine, her stride languid like that of royalty. "You should keep your doors locked," she said again.

"Thanks." Karen nodded, cutting her eyes uneasily to the nearest window. "I'll do that."

CHAPTER THREE

Tristan didn't normally like to use his telepathy to deliberately manipulate humans, but there were some instances in which he found it to be a necessary evil.

"I really appreciate your help," he told the pharmacy assistant with a smile.

"It's no problem at all, Mr. Noble," she replied, color rising in her cheeks as she handed him a white paper sack. "Two thirty-day bottles of bupropion."

As a physician, he couldn't write prescriptions for himself, but he *could* pretend to be Brandon. When he'd handed the assistant his driver's license, he'd used his power to trick her into seeing Brandon's name on the laminated card, not his own. The illusion had been so perfect, her persuasion so complete, she hadn't looked twice or doubted his identity once.

On the way back to the clinic, he thought about stopping by Karen's house, to try to explain things, make amends by her somehow. The trip into town hadn't taken more than an hour, round trip, including a swing through

Starbucks on the way back for a Venti bold with a double shot, no room. The coffee was hotter than hell, and he sipped at it warily along the drive. As he tried for a drink while maneuvering along the winding, rutted gravel road leading up to the Morin compound, he hit a particularly deep pothole that rocked the Jeep on its suspension, sending a hot splatter of coffee down the front of his face and coat, splashing onto the leg of his jeans.

"Shit!" Driving with one hand, letting the Jeep weave precariously close to the shoulder of the road, he shoved the paper cup into the nearest console tray, then raised his hips, trying to pull the soaked denim off his skin before it scalded too badly.

In doing so, he cut his eyes off the road momentarily, no more than a few seconds. When he glanced back up through the windshield again, he saw a car pulling out of one of the side drives ahead of him, merging unexpectedly onto the compound's main road.

"Holy shit!" He slammed on his brakes. The wheels of the Jeep abruptly locked, sending the heavy truck skidding sideways in the gravel. It bounced heavily over the shoulder, sending more coffee splattering, and crashed grille-first into the broad trunk of a venerable pine tree. The airbag deployed, slamming into his torso as it abruptly inflated, stunning the breath and wits from him.

With a groan, he blinked dazedly, watching pinpoints of light sparkle and dance in front of him against a backdrop of heavy white nylon. Already, the airbag was deflating, growing lax in front of him, and he reached for his seat belt.

"Shit." He was shaking uncontrollably, adrenaline surging through him. As he glanced through the side mirror, he could see the car he'd damn near hit and bit back another groan.

"Shit," he muttered again, because his grandfather was getting out of the black Mercedes sedan, slamming the door furiously and then stomping toward Tristan's Jeep.

"Hey, Michel." Bracing himself for what he felt sure would be an ass chewing, he opened the driver's side door and stumbled out. His neck and back felt stiff and sore, and he wondered if he'd suffered whiplash at the impact.

"What the hell's wrong with you?" Michel demanded, his brows knitted deeply, his hands balled into fists. "You could have killed us both!"

"I'm sorry. I just looked away for a second. I was trying to—"

"Where have you been? I've been calling and calling."

"What?" Tristan shook his head, still somewhat dazed from smacking face-first into the airbag.

"Why isn't your cell phone on?" Michel snapped.

"It is..." Tristan began, reaching for the clip on the waist of his jeans where he customarily holstered his phone. To his surprise, it was empty. He racked his brain back through the morning's events, then realized... "I left it at home."

"You're supposed to be at the clinic."

"I was there. I had to run an errand in town. I'm just on my way back now." It occurred to Tristan that even though Michel was wound up about something, it had nothing to do with their narrowly averted headlong collision. His grandfather's eyes were round, his pupils enlarged, his scent tinged with the heavy aroma of adrenaline and anxious sweat. "What's going on?"

"I thought something was wrong," Michel said. "I thought something had happened to you."

Tristan managed a laugh, convinced that he'd struck his head harder than he'd first suspected and that he was having some kind of auditory hallucination. *What the hell could've happened?* he wondered. *An overdose of boredom?*

At this, the cleft between Michel's brows deepened. "You're supposed to be at the clinic," he seethed again. "Eleanor could have fallen or cut herself. What if she'd started to hemorrhage? I would have needed you to bring me the clotting treatment."

Eleanor Noble, Brandon's grandmother, had been diagnosed three years earlier with what Michel called *autoimmune-specific disseminated intravascular coagulopathy*. It was a congenital disease unique among full-blooded Brethren. Michel had long hypothesized that the disease was the result of centuries of inbreeding among various Brethren clans, a practice dating as far back as the fourteenth century, when their ancestors had lived in medieval France. Though the Brethren Elders had tried to take great care to prevent direct blood relations from intermarrying, there had been no way to prevent it completely in such a closed breeding environment. It was extremely rare, affecting about one in every thousand Brethren adults.

Sufferers of the disease eventually came to exhaust their platelet supply, the chief component that allowed for blood clotting and coagulation. Normally a healthy individual's platelets were replenished regularly by the bone marrow, but in Eleanor, this process had become irregular, sporadic, and ineffective. Without regular infusions of new platelets and a synthesized clotting factor that Michel's medical research company, Pharmaceaux International, had developed, Eleanor would eventually bleed at the slightest injury or touch.

"Do you understand how serious that would have been?" Michel demanded of him, his face flushed angrily.

Of course I understand. Tristan bit back the sharp reply, furrowing his brows. *I watched my mother die from the same goddamn thing.*

"She could bleed to death," Michel supplied—even though, as the one who'd presided over Lisette's funeral service the day before, he was perfectly aware of Tristan's all too personal familiarity with the disease.

"I'm sorry." Angry, embarrassed, and most of all, ashamed—because he liked Eleanor and would have been beside himself with grief and guilt if anything had happened to her—Tristan looked away. "I wasn't gone long, Michel. I swear. I just—"

"You were supposed to be at the clinic." Michel fairly spat the words this time, jabbing his forefinger in the air at Tristan's nose with forceful emphasis. "No place else."

"There was nothing going on," Tristan argued, bristling. "I thought it would be all right. I'm sorry, I said. It won't happen again."

For a long moment, Michel stood there, looking for all the world like he was toying with the idea of punching Tristan. Then he turned, stomping toward the Jeep. "You're goddamn right it won't."

As Tristan watched, Michel opened the driver's door, leaned inside, and snatched his keys from the ignition.

"What are you doing?" he asked. "Are you kidding? You're taking away my keys?"

He started to laugh and Michel shot him a withering glare. "These aren't yours," he said, holding up the keys, letting them dangle in the air between them. "They're *mine*. I bought and paid for them."

At that, something in Tristan snapped. His day had been nothing but a topsy-turvy, bewildering maelstrom of miserable, conflicting emotions, and all at once, he'd had enough. "Yeah. I know. You never let me forget it, do you? Just like you never let Mom—or anyone else—forget we were both only here by your say-so, your goddamn okay."

Michel had been walking back toward his car, but his footsteps came to a crunching halt now in the loose gravel. His eyes narrowed into furious slits as he glanced over his shoulder. "*Quoi?*" he asked quietly, almost incredulously, reverting in his rage to his native French. "What did you say to me?"

"You heard me." Squaring off against his grandfather, Tristan bared his fists. "Tell me something, Michel. How long did it take for you to decide which one got your precious clotting treatment—Eleanor or my mom?"

Only Eleanor had received the regimens of clotting factor. Although she and Lisette had been diagnosed within weeks of each other, Eleanor's had come as the result of her husband—Michel's best friend—Augustus contacting Michel by mail for help. Lisette had already been at Lake Tahoe, already in the Brethren medical clinic by the time Augustus and Michel had been able to smuggle Eleanor out of Kentucky. By the time Eleanor had arrived among the Morins, Lisette had already suffered the massive cranial hemorrhage that had incapacitated her.

"I would have helped your mother if I'd been able," Michel told him.

Tristan managed a laugh. "Bullshit. The clotting serum might have stopped the bleeding in her brain in time."

"Tristan," Michel said, his furious expression faltering. "There was nothing I could do. Even if we'd been able to somehow stop the bleeding, she still wouldn't have—"

"You don't know that," Tristan snapped. "You didn't even try. You probably thought she had it coming. Hell, I know most of the rest of the clan did."

Michel's mouth drew down angrily again. "That isn't—"

"What?" Tristan cut in. "True? Of course it is. Why don't you just admit it for once? You thought she was a whore."

Michel's hand flew so quickly, Tristan didn't even see the blow coming. His grandfather slapped him hard enough to snap his head to the side, leaving a bright, aching spot high on the crest of his cheekbone.

"Don't you ever say that about your mother again," Michel said in a low, angry voice. "And don't you dare presume to tell me what I do or do not think."

Tristan's birth father, Arnaud Morin, had been Michel's son. Lisette had been married to Arnaud's brother, Phillip, but the two had enjoyed a short-lived but apparently passionate fling together. Arnaud had committed suicide, leaving Lisette to deal with the fallout once the affair had been discovered.

"The only reason you didn't kick Mom out of the compound was because you found out she was pregnant with me—Arnaud's bastard son," he snapped at Michel.

"Those are your words, not mine. I've never thought of you like that," Michel said. "None of us have."

"Yeah, I could see how much the whole family gave a shit by how many showed up for her funeral yesterday. Counting you, me, and Mason, that made, what? A dozen? No, wait, three of them were Nobles, and two—Karen and Lina—were human." Idiotically, he felt on the verge of tears again. Part of the stress he'd felt yesterday that had forced him into bed with Karen were the shame and dismay that came with the realization of just how empty his mother's graveside had been. Staring at Michel, he pleaded, "Is that why you didn't want me to marry Tessa Noble?"

"This doesn't have anything to do with Tessa. You weren't in love with her, anyway. And she's in love with your brother."

"Rene's my *half* brother. And he's half human. He and Naima both. Does that make them better than me somehow to you? They're bastards too, but hey, at least they're half-breeds and didn't spoil your otherwise spotless bloodline."

Michel blinked at him, then shook his head. "Is that what you think?"

"Am I wrong?" Tristan shot back.

"I've never treated you differently than anyone else in this family."

"Bullshit! I don't see any of the other grandchildren trapped here like I am. Hell, you let everyone else in the clan come and go as they damn well please."

"Trapped?" Michel bristled visibly at this. *"Mon Dieu,* you are the most ungrateful, self-centered, spoiled—"

Tristan laughed. "Are you kidding me?"

"I've given you an education, a vocation, a home, a career—anything you could ever want," Michel shouted.

"You don't know what I want," Tristan yelled back. "You son of a bitch, you've never even bothered to ask!" Without waiting for Michel to react or respond, he turned around and began to walk away.

"Keep your keys and your goddamn Jeep," Tristan said without turning around. "If you'd given half the shit about my mother—and me—that you do about Eleanor, she might still be alive today."

****

After Naima left, Karen moved methodically throughout her house, making sure all the doors and windows were locked. The idea that Jean Luc Davenant might still be out in the surrounding woods troubled her.

"Don't be afraid," Naima had said, trying to smile in reassuring fashion as she'd walked down the front steps. "We'll find him."

Don't be afraid. Yeah, right. Karen sat at the breakfast bar in her bathrobe, her hair still damp, cradling a cup of coffee between her hands. Like Tristan's, her house had an open first-story floor plan, with the far wall made of floor-to-ceiling windows and sliding glass doors. She'd always loved the view these provided, but now felt exposed and vulnerable.

A hint of movement among the trees along the periphery of the yard caught her attention. She cut her gaze to track it and spied a shadow-draped figure, oblong and indistinct, behind a cluster of pine trunks. Her breath drew to a halt, her eyes flew wide, her entire body growing rigid in her chair.

Michel thinks he'll be back. And that he won't be alone this time.

Naima's warning echoing in her mind, Karen slowly lowered her mug to the countertop. Inching her hips sideways, she eased herself toward the edge of the seat, letting her feet drop slowly, deliberately to the floor. She kept her eyes glued to that strange shape in the trees as she made her way from the kitchen to a nearby linen closet. *It's just a trick of the light,* she kept trying to tell herself. *There's no one out there. Naima was just here. She would've sensed it if Davenant was close by.*

But Naima had speculated that the reason Jean Luc had been able to infiltrate so deeply into the Morin compound undetected the night before was that he was a Brethren. They were used to sensing each other in the area, to the point where they pretty much tuned out the awareness. Unless they probed more deeply, looking for something Naima called "unfamiliar mental imprints" with their telepathy, they might not realize immediately if there was a stranger among them.

Without turning her back to the windows, Karen opened the closet door. She reached inside, fingers groping blindly until she found the light switch, flipped it on. In the corner, she kept a loaded Browning .257 Roberts rifle. Her father had taught her to shoot when she'd been no more than ten, and she kept in practice.

Hefting the gun from its corner, she reached for the shelf where she kept her ammunition. As she loaded the rifle, she kept her eyes trained ahead, past the closet threshold and across the living room, out the windows and into the trees.

Is it moving? Is that a person or a tree branch? What if it's Tristan?

"Good," she muttered, chambering a round. "I want to shoot him right about now too."

Feigning courage she didn't necessarily feel, Karen boldly crossed the main floor of her house. She'd left a pair of weather-beaten hiking boots by the back door at some point, and stepped into them now, leaving them unlaced. Pushing open the sliding glass, she walked outside, feeling the crisp, chilly air immediately bite into her skin.

Her breath frosted around her face, and within seconds, her back teeth began to chatter. With a frown, Karen started across the yard, her boots clomping heavily in the thick carpeting of dried pine needles underfoot.

"I see you," she tried to shout, but all at once, her windpipe felt like it had collapsed in on itself, shriveling down to a pin-hole circumference, and her voice came out hoarse, little more than a croak. She cleared her throat and tried again, hefting the rifle to her shoulder and narrowing her gaze down the sight. "Who's out there?"

The grinding crunch of tire treads through gravel from somewhere behind startled her, and she whirled. An enormous black SUV, all glossy black paint and sparkling chrome trim, pulled down the narrow drive approaching her house—a Cadillac Escalade with a front vanity tag that read *TOP DOC*. The big truck came to a stop facing her, the engine rumbling to a halt.

Karen turned, looking back toward the trees, but the shadowy figure hiding there was gone. A lone, low-hanging bough swished in the slim space where she thought she'd seen it, as if stirred by an otherwise indiscernible breeze.

"Do you always take up target practice in your bathrobe?" a man asked with a laugh as he opened the driver's side door and stepped out of the cab. Tall and lean, he wore his coal black hair combed back from his face, the slim hint of a goatee on his chin. Dressed in mirrored sunglasses, black leather pants, and a double-breasted wool overcoat, he looked for all the world like some kind of goth rock superstar or Hollywood actor stepping out for his latest premier.

"Mason?" Because she was too surprised and bewildered to react at first, she kept the rifle stock raised.

"Don't shoot." He held up his hands in mock surrender. In one, he held a paper sack with the words *Lake Tahoe Bakery & Gourmet* printed across the front. "I come bearing scones."

****

As Tristan followed the road toward the small, two-room guest cottage in which Brandon and Lina had been staying, he passed Karen's place. To his surprise, he saw his uncle Mason's black Cadillac truck in the driveway, and thus cut a wide berth through the woods to avoid them. Despite this, he could smell her, the sweet, tantalizing hint of her fragrance wafting in the breeze.

Goddamn it, he thought, because he could feel his gums begin to throb at this, a low-grade but insistent ache. Had he thought on the drive home that he'd be able to just walk up to her front door without any problems? Talk to her— stand in front of her, for Christ's sake—without the bloodlust ruining everything again? When had things ever been that easy where Karen was concerned?

Hunching his shoulders, he shoved his hands deep into his pockets. He meant to hurry on his way but blinked when he felt the paper bag with Brandon's medicine.

I was able to keep it under control, Brandon had told him of his own bloodlust, and of using the Wellbutrin to curb his Brethren appetites.

I can't take this anymore, Tristan thought, because even though he clung to his Brethren heritage with a fierce, nearly relentless sort of pride, he hated it too, hated being like his grandfather with a deep-seated, festering vehemence.

He drew the bag from his pocket, then removed one of the bottles. Popping the cap, he brought it to his mouth and tipped his head back, letting a mouthful of the pills tumble against his tongue.

Brandon takes two of these a day, three hundred milligrams, he said, to control the bloodlust, he thought. But like most antidepressants, it could take several weeks to build up enough of a therapeutic dose to feel any effects. If you were human, that is. With his accelerated healing abilities, as a Brethren, Tristan could also metabolize medications much more rapidly, and he hoped that by glutting himself on at least half the pills at once, he'd feel the calming effects on the bloodlust right away.

With a grimace, he choked the first bunch down, then glanced over his shoulder through the trees toward Karen's house. It lay behind him now, but still, that lingering hint of her remained discernable to him, tantalizing.

Another handful, another wince, and another quick swallow, and he figured it would be enough. *It has to be.*

When he reached Brandon and Lina's house, he saw a rental car idling in the driveway, the trunk open as Brandon lugged out an armload of overstuffed luggage. He caught sight of Tristan approaching and smiled, visibly puzzled to find him on foot.

Where's your truck? he asked.

Long story. Tristan shook his head, dismissive. *Hey, I've got a going-away gift for you.*

He tossed Brandon one of the medicine bottles, keeping the other for himself with only the slightest hint of guilt. *Because I need them too,* he thought. *More than anyone, Brandon would understand.*

Brandon caught the bottle easily, one-handed.

I could only get you a one-month supply, Tristan lied, affecting the appropriate mental tone and facial affect of regret. *But if you need more, let me know, and I'll call in a prescription for you to a pharmacy down there, okay?*

Brandon nodded, striding forward to meet Tristan, his hand outstretched. *Thanks, Dr. Morin,* he said. *For everything.*

No, Brandon. He accepted the younger man's proffered shake. *Thank* you.

CHAPTER FOUR

When he finally made it back to his house, he was stiff, sore, and not at all surprised to find his uncle's SUV parked at the end of his drive. After all, he'd seen Mason at Karen's less than thirty minutes earlier, and as Michel's eldest son, there had been more than enough time and opportunity for him to catch wind of Tristan's crash.

"I don't want to talk about it," he growled, tromping up the steps past where Mason sat waiting for him, cheery grin plastered on his face despite the cold.

"About what?" Mason asked, his voice deceptively innocent and oblivious. He'd been smoking a clove cigarette, the aromatic smoke enveloping him in a spicy cloud, but snuffed it now beneath the toe of his boot.

"Exactly." Tristan shoved his front door open, grateful that he hadn't locked up when he'd left, considering his house keys were now officially in his grandfather's possession.

Mason followed him inside. A prominent plastic surgeon based in Los Angeles, he looked every bit the part of a successful physician who made his living doing breast implants, rhinoplasties, liposuction, and facelifts on the rich and famous. Mason was just as physically perfect as any of his exclusive clientele. His youthful appearance pegged him as a man in his mid- to late-thirties, tops, when in fact, he was more than two hundred years old.

"Pack a bag," Mason said as Tristan shrugged his way out of his coat.

This was a game Mason would play when Tristan had been a boy. He'd surprise Tristan and Lisette by arriving unannounced to whisk them both away to Las Vegas or New York or maybe Chicago, London, or Paris. Mason had always been very enigmatic about these trips, telling Tristan and his mother to each "pack a bag" with only those items they couldn't live without. "Everything else," he'd always say, "we can buy once we're on our way."

The excursions had always been as much to benefit Mason as Tristan and Lisette. While Mason had never made a secret of his sexual predilections, he'd never publicly admitted them either, at least to his family. But during their trips abroad he'd introduced Tristan and Lisette to at least a half dozen or so "uncles" of one sort or another who would accompany them—all of them human, and none of them of any true blood kin.

"Not today, Mason," Tristan said, tossing his coat onto the back of the couch. Was it just his imagination, or could he still detect Karen's scent in the house, despite the fact he'd burned her blouse? With a frown, he sniffed.

"Yes, today," Mason replied with a laugh, shrugging back the heavy sleeve of his wool overcoat enough to check his watch. As he moved, Karen's fragrance stirred, and Tristan realized this was what he'd been smelling; he'd been in Karen's house long enough for her scent to seep into his clothes. "Right now, as a matter of fact. We're late."

With a heavy sigh, Tristan turned to him. "Look, I'm really not having a good day," he began wearily.

"I know." Still smiling, Mason held out his hand in invitation. "Which is why you really need to come with me."

****

Karen sifted through her travel bag, ticking items off her mental inventory for at least the hundredth time. *Toothpaste? Check. Toothbrush? Check. Deodorant, perfume, hairspray? Check, check, and check.*

Mason had been very specific in his instructions, but at the same time bafflingly mysterious. "Pack a bag," he'd told her as he'd walked out the door, leaving her to feel as if she was now in the midst of some mischievous well-planned game, one in which she was not privy to all the rules. "Travel lightly—only items you can't live without. Anything else we can buy along the way."

She'd dressed in blue jeans, boots, and a sweater, drawing her hair back in a loosely fitted clip at the nape of her neck. Dancing down the steps from her bedroom loft two at a time, she found herself cutting a wary glance out the window toward the trees, then shook her head.

Stop it, she told herself. *There's no one out there. It was a trick of the light, shadows beneath the tree limbs. I was imagining things.*

She'd returned the rifle to her linen closet but hadn't quite convinced herself enough to unload it. *Just in case,* she'd thought.

"I'm supposed to be at the clinic tonight," she'd protested to Mason.

"It's taken care of," he'd replied.

"But Eleanor has her treatment first thing tomorrow morning," she'd said. "I need to let Michel know if I can't—"

Still smiling in that enigmatic fashion, he'd gently cut her short. "It's taken care of."

A horn sounded from outside; Mason had returned. Feeling nervous and excited, Karen grabbed her purse and hurried for the door. Between her humiliating one-night stand with Tristan and the idea that one of the Davenants might be on the prowl, getting the hell away from South Lake Tahoe sounded like just what the doctor had ordered. Ducking outside, she let the front door swing shut behind her, then turned, using her key to turn the deadbolt home.

****

"Where are you going?" Tristan leaned forward, blinking stupidly out the window as Mason turned down Karen's driveway.

"Quick detour," Mason replied, pulling to a stop beside her house. He leaned across the cab, arm outstretched, and opened the passenger door beside Tristan. "Climb in back, would you, *mon lapin?*"

Tristan's bewilderment turned to anxiety, then alarm. "Why?"

"Because it's good manners to offer the lady shotgun." With a smile, Mason pressed his hand against the steering column, blatting the horn in beckon.

Tristan sat, paralyzed in his seat, a grim sort of realization dawning on him, and after a few moments, he saw Karen step out the front door, a traveling bag hanging from her shoulder. Stricken, he turned to his uncle, and when he found Mason still wearing that goddamn Cheshire Cat grin, he bristled.

"No," he said, shoving his door open wider. "No, no, no, hell no."

He hopped out of the truck and wrenched open the back door, seizing his own bag by the strap. Karen caught sight of him as she came down the stairs, and her footsteps skittered to a halt in the loose dirt and gravel, her blue eyes growing round and uncertain.

Her heart jackhammered beneath her sweater. He could hear it, goddamn it; he could sense it in his mind, could smell the sudden surge of anxious adrenaline in her bloodstream as her body tensed reflexively for fight or flight.

"Let me take that bag for you." Mason had obviously misinterpreted Tristan's hesitation as having changed his mind, and he climbed out of the truck to approach Karen, arms outstretched. He paused long enough to kiss her in the continental fashion, leaning forward, brushing his lips quickly, lightly against either cheek. "Hop in. Your chariot awaits."

"Mason, I..." she began, glancing between him and Tristan, looking for all the world like a rabbit cornered between a pair of hounds. Her face had become drained of color save for two bright patches of nearly fluorescent blush that had bloomed in the high apples of her cheeks. "I...I don't think I should..."

"Be carrying your own luggage? Of course not," Mason interjected mildly, slipping the bag from her shoulder. "That's why I offered to do it for you."

Leaving her to sputter, rooted in place, he carried her bag to the Escalade.

You tricked me. Tristan locked eyes with Mason, his brows narrowing.

I did, yes, Mason replied, catching Tristan off guard with his utter lack of protest. He leaned past his nephew to toss Karen's bag into the truck.

Tristan caught him by the sleeve. "I'm not going," he said in a low, angry voice.

Mason ignored him completely, returning instead to Karen's side. As he led her toward the passenger side, she stared at Tristan in visible apprehension. The bloodlust still did not stir within him, but something else did—shame.

Because she hates me now, he realized glumly. *She probably thinks I'm some kind of major asshole. And she's right.*

Lowering his eyes to the ground, he pressed his lips together in a thin line. He listened to the soft rustle of her clothes as she drew near, then stepped up into the cab. The leather-upholstered seats creaked faintly as she sat down; then, with a sharp snap of wind and a trailing click, the door shut behind her.

"Let's go, *mon lapin,*" Mason said as he returned to the driver's side. "I told you before—we're running late."

This had been his nickname for Tristan when he'd been younger—*mon lapin,* or *my rabbit* in his native French. He said nothing more, merely climbed in and shut his door.

For what? Tristan asked.

Mason pivoted in his seat to look back through the opened doorway at him. *You'll see,* he replied with a wink and a smile. *Come on, now. Get in.*

****

It wasn't a long trip to the Reno airport, but for Karen, it seemed to take an eternity. Throughout the entire ride, she sat rigidly in her seat, her hands folded in the nest of her lap. Although Mason chattered the whole way, making idle and friendly conversation into which she'd occasionally interject a murmured acknowledgment or sound of feigned interest, she focused more on Tristan. She could see him through the rearview mirror as he sat, equally stiff-backed and uncomfortable behind her, his arms crossed, his brows furrowed sullenly, his gaze averted out the window.

She'd almost turned around and darted back into her house when she'd seen him step out of Mason's truck. Why she hadn't done so still remained as much a mystery to her as their ultimate destination or the purpose of the trip Mason had orchestrated.

I want to go home, she thought, looking out her window, seeing Tristan's morose and distant gaze fixed outwardly through the side mirror. *Not just back to my house at the compound, but* home *as in Kansas. As in back to my parents' house, my old room upstairs. Under the blankets, head beneath the pillow, never coming out.*

58

"Have you ever heard of the Trésor?" Mason asked, drawing her from her thoughts. "It's a brand-new casino resort, the grandest in Las Vegas. Not to mention the largest, most expensive ever built in the country."

Not one much for gambling, Karen shook her head. "Is that where we're going?"

With a grin, Mason nodded. He shifted his weight, reaching beneath his coat lapel to produce a small, cream-colored card with gold embossed scripting. It was an invitation, she saw, as he handed it to her, for the resort's grand-opening celebration.

"I've got three VIP suites waiting for us, and tonight, we're to arrive fashionably late for the official soiree, sometime after ten."

From the backseat, Tristan made a sound. It might have been a snicker, but she couldn't be sure. "Good luck with that," he remarked drily. "It's a seven-hour drive to Vegas from here."

"At least," Mason agreed. "Which is why we're going to fly, not drive." When at last, Tristan cut his eyes away from the window to blink at his uncle in surprise, Mason chuckled. "Come on, *mon lapin*," he said. "You think Michel's the only one who can afford to charter a plane in this family?"

CHAPTER FIVE

It worked, Tristan thought, surprised and admittedly impressed. *I'll be goddamned. Brandon was right.*

Throughout the ride on the way to the airport—trapped in the cramped confines of the Escalade's cab—he'd waited anxiously for the wondrous, intoxicating aroma that was surely radiating from Karen in heady waves to hit him, overwhelm him, cause the bloodlust in him to stir with brutal, relentless insistence. To his surprise—his utter amazement, in fact—it had not. Even now, hours after taking the Wellbutrin pills, he sat in the cabin of the small Hawker jet Mason had chartered for their trip to Vegas and felt no hint.

I can't believe it, he thought, and he couldn't help but grin as he looked out the window and into the impenetrable wall of clouds visible at their cruising altitude.

Tristan sat at the aft end of the cabin, while at the forward end, Mason and Karen sat across from each other. It occurred to him that he could open his mind, sense her thoughts, make himself privy through her to whatever quiet conversations she and his uncle had been sharing throughout the duration of the flight so far. But when he tried, he felt a peculiar, unfamiliar sensation. Instead of a sudden flood of thoughts, memories and emotions from Karen's mind, all he sensed was the mental equivalent of what he could see outside his window—nothing but clouds.

Huh. With a frown, he closed his eyes, pressing his fingertips to his brow. Concentrating this time, he tried to force his way through the sensory fog, but it did not good.

The medicine must have dampened my telepathy too, he realized, remembering all too late: *Didn't Brandon tell me while he lived on the farm in Kentucky his telepathy never seemed to work well?*

"Are you okay?"

He opened his eyes to find Mason standing in front of him. He'd stripped off his overcoat and blazer and turned back the sleeves on his black silk shirt. In one hand, he cradled a crystal tumbler loaded with ice, filled to three-quarter capacity with a drink Tristan strongly suspected, given his uncle's preferences, was a martini. Shaken, not stirred, just like in the James Bond movies. Mason preferred them with almond-stuffed Queen olives, and a hint of green tucked among the ice cubes suggested that his chartered flight crew had been sure to stock them on board.

"You were holding your head just now," Mason said. "Are you feeling all right?"

For the first time in his entire life, Tristan could only wonder about another person's thoughts. As with Karen, when he tried to open his mind to Mason, there was nothing but haze.

"I...I'm fine. Just the altitude, I think." He glanced past Mason toward Karen's seat, but it was conspicuously empty.

"She's gone to the lavatory," Mason said, following his gaze. As he settled himself comfortably against the couch beside his nephew, he reached out, patting Tristan's knee. "Are you finished sulking now? Ready to be sociable?"

Tristan shot him a glower. "I haven't been sulking. I'm pissed at you."

Mason laughed. "What on earth for?"

"Because you know what happens whenever I'm with her," Tristan snapped, sparing another cautious look toward the cabin front. "You know how she makes me feel."

Mason laughed again. "Tristan, you're being ridiculous. How on earth have you managed to work with the woman at the clinic for the past year if it's so impossible to be around her?"

"That's different. Taking care of Mom distracted me. And I didn't say it was impossible."

"Do you honestly expect me to believe that the two of you never interacted except to care for Lisette? You never talk to her? Never ask about the weather, offer to buy her a cup of coffee, for God's sake?"

"Of course I do. But at the clinic, if it gets too much, I can get away. I have an office I can go to. I can close the door." Brows furrowed, Tristan leaned forward, seething, "I'm not trapped in a goddamn jet fifty thousand feet up in the air with her."

"What makes you think I'm trying to trap you?" Mason looked amused but wounded. "And why do you think my inviting Karen has anything to do with *you* in the first place? Really, Tristan. The world doesn't always revolve around—"

"If you didn't bring her along just to piss me off, then why did you?"

Mason's expression grew uncharacteristically solemn. "Because the compound's no place for her to be right now."

"What do you mean?" Tristan asked.

"Have you talked to Naima today?" Mason asked, and when Tristan shook his head, he continued. "Your grandfather?"

"You mean, outside of having him chew me a new ass for leaving the clinic for a couple of hours without his express, written permission? No."

Mason studied him a long moment. "They found one of the Davenants in the woods last night."

"What?" Tristan blinked in surprise.

Mason nodded grimly. "*Oui.* His name is Jean Luc. I knew him once, a long time ago, before the flight from Kentucky. He used to amuse himself by stringing cats upside down from the trees and partially eviscerating them to see how long they could survive...and if they'd resort to eating their own guts to do it."

Tristan grimaced. "Nice."

"Oh yes," Mason agreed. "He's got a grudge against Michel on account of the fact that he treated Augustus Noble's injuries, not Victor Davenant's, after their duel to win Eleanor's hand. Judging by the fact he tried to kill Naima and Michel with his bare hands, I'm guessing he hasn't changed his mindset too much in the last two hundred years." He leaned forward and added in a low voice, "Michel asked me to take Karen away from the grounds for a while. At least until he and Naima can track the gentleman down, make sure he can't cause any more mischief."

"Why specifically Karen?" Tristan asked, puzzled.

The corner of Mason's mouth hooked in a crooked smile. Tipping his head back, he drained his martini in a long, single swallow. The ice cubes tinkled together as he set the glass aside.

"My dear rabbit," he said, patting Tristan's cheek, his palm damp and cool with residual moisture. "Part of the reason our clan broke away from the Kentucky Brethren was that we didn't believe that humans should be our primary source of blood nourishment. The Davenants were among those who didn't agree."

Realizing what he meant, Tristan bristled, his brows narrowing, his gaze automatically darting toward the front of the cabin, even though Karen had yet to return from the bathroom. "He was going after her."

"They think so, yes," Mason said quietly. "They think he'd been hiding out for at least a day in the woods near her house."

"That son of a bitch," Tristan seethed, closing his hands into fists. *He probably watched her all day—followed her to the funeral, then to my house. He was probably in the woods the whole goddamn time, watching through the windows...watching us together...*

"You should have told me back in Tahoe," he said to Mason. "I could've helped Michel and Naima search the woods, hunt the bastard down. I could have..."

Mason chuckled, and Tristan's voice faltered. "What?" he asked, but Mason shook his head. "What?"

"Nothing." Mason shook his head again, glancing up as the flight attendant stepped into the main cabin and approached. "You just sound like a man in love, that's all."

"What?" Tristan blinked. "Bullshit. That... I just... That's complete bullshit. I'm not..."

While he continued to sputter, Mason held out his empty glass to the attendant. "Another, Dr. Morin?" she asked with a courteous smile.

"That would be divine, my dear," Mason replied. "Thank you."

"For you, Dr. Morin?" The attendant turned that sparkling smile in Tristan's direction.

"Yeah." Suddenly, getting drunk didn't sound unappealing. "I'll take a Jack and Coke." Because shit-faced didn't sound too bad either, he added quickly, "A double."

With a demure nod, she turned and walked away. Watching the sashay of her hips beneath her uniform slacks as if he had half an interest, Mason remarked, "So have you fed from Karen yet?"

Tristan choked. "What? No. Are you crazy? God, no." At this, Mason laughed loud enough to attract the stewardess's curious attention before she ducked into the galley, and humiliated, Tristan fumed. "What's so goddamn funny?"

"You are, *mon lapin.*" With a soft groan, Mason stood, stretching his back, languid and graceful as a cat. He smiled as he reached down, tousling Tristan's hair fondly. "You are."

****

With a groan, Karen pawed the button alongside the lavatory toilet to flush it, sending a thin puddle of vomit down the stainless steel drain with an abrupt flood of bright blue, chemically treated water.

"God," she said, her voice ragged as she pivoted and caught sight of herself in the vanity mirror above the sink.

Her face was a ghastly shade of pale, broken only by the stark, rosy splotches of her cheeks and the constellations of freckles splayed across her forehead and nose. Her makeup had smeared beneath her eyes when she'd retched, and she leaned closer, blotting at them with her fingertips, trying to wipe away the ruined eyeliner.

Terrific, she thought. It was a four-hour flight, and every moment of it thus far had been an exercise in anxiety control for her. It wasn't that she didn't like to fly. *It's the landing you have to watch out for,* she thought grimly as she rinsed her mouth out with water. *And the fall in between.*

She'd only ever been on a plane once before in her life, and she'd spent most of that trip either hanging over the commode or face-first in the complimentary airsick bag she'd found tucked in the seatback pocket in front of her. She loathed the idea of air travel so much, she'd even made the grueling move from her native Kansas west to Nevada by land, with the beat-up Mustang she still owned to that day and a U-Haul trailer hitched to the back.

"Are you all right?" Mason had asked her gently upon takeoff, as she'd gripped the dove-gray leather arms of her seat with white-knuckled ferocity.

She'd forced a smile. "Terrific," she'd croaked.

To his credit, he'd managed to distract her for much of the flight by talking to her, telling her how once upon a time, he'd jetted Tristan and his mother off on numerous such whirlwind, globe-trotting adventures. She enjoyed hearing stories about Tristan as a boy; his past was something he spoke little of, at least around her, and she'd often suspected that grief and regret over his mother's illness were to blame.

"Of course, some of the others would whisper about it, all of the trips we'd take," Mason had confided, leaning close enough to speak into her ear, his voice low, a nearly conspiratorial tone. "I'm sure plenty of my kith and kin thought we were sleeping together, me and Lisette."

"She *was* a beautiful woman, after all," Karen had observed, because she'd seen photographs of Lisette from before her illness had struck.

"She was, yes." Mason had nodded. "Inside and out. But I've never been one to find fancy with my own species." When she'd looked puzzled at this, he'd chuckled. "Don't tell me Michel's never gotten drunk enough around you to tell you all about his theories on Brethren pair-bonds. No? Well, then, my darling, you are in for a treat." At this, he'd caught sight of their flight attendant as she passed through the cabin, and had flagged her to order a martini.

"Michel hates things he can't reasonably explain," Mason had said once his drink arrived. He'd stirred it with his pinkie, swirling the ice cubes musically together before taking a sip. "Love being first and foremost among them. According to him, there are Brethren who are genetically predisposed to be attracted to, and mate with, other

Brethren. They're breeders, as he calls them, the ones who keep our genetic lines intact. Like Augustus and Eleanor Noble. They're inherently meant to be together. As for the rest of us..."

Another sip, another finger dip, and this time, he'd hooked the enormous olive that bobbed among the ice chips. Popping it into his mouth, he closed his eyes, his expression growing wistful as if he savored it, then began to chew.

"As for the rest of us, Michel thinks we're meant to breed with humans. *Pair-bonding,* he calls it—an inherent attraction by which certain humans and Brethren are biologically, psychologically and telepathically meant to be together."

Pair-bonding, Karen thought as she looked at herself in the bathroom mirror. According to Mason, Michel had hypothesized that the proverbial deal would be ultimately sealed by the act of a Brethren feeding from the human to whom he felt this undeniable attraction.

"He said it had something to do with the dopamine-mediated reward pathways in both partner's brains," Mason had said. "Some sort of prohormone precursor likely synthesized in the hypothalamus and regulated by the posterior pituitary gland." He'd had several martinis by this point, enough so that even with his naturally accelerated metabolism, he'd clearly felt a pleasant little buzz, and with a flap of his hand and a laugh, he'd added, "Or some such bullshit."

Whatever the science behind it, whatever the cause, Mason had said that once the Brethren fed from the human to whom he or she was pair-bonded, an infallible mental rapport was established between the two.

"How did Michel come up with an idea like that?" Karen had wondered aloud, unable to help herself, and stealing a backward glance toward the rear of the compartment, where Tristan sat by himself, glowering out the window.

"I don't know," Mason had admitted, and when she'd looked back in his direction, she'd blushed brightly because he'd noticed her distraction. "But I think it may stem from something he observed on a personal level, if you know what I mean."

Karen had blinked in surprise, because she'd never known Michel to be in love with anyone before, Brethren or human. He'd had multiple wives once upon a time, before the Morins fled from Kentucky, because Brethren law had mandated polygamy for its male members. They'd all been Brethren women, however, and Michel had apparently turned all of them loose once they'd arrived in California. He'd lived for a time with Eleanor Noble when she'd come to stay with them, but to Karen's knowledge, there had never been any romantic involvement between them.

Then—and now, in the lavatory—she racked her brain trying to imagine who Michel might have loved enough to question his entire genetic predisposition. Then and now, she found she had no earthly idea.

But if it's true about pair-bonding, she thought, *could that explain how I feel about Tristan? How I've felt drawn to him from the start?*

And could it also explain what happened last night—why he wouldn't feed from me? If Mason knows about Michel's pair-bonding theory, surely Tristan does too. Maybe he feels it too, that we're supposed to be that way—pair-bonded—but he doesn't want it.

Turning her eyes away from the mirror, Karen blinked against the dim sting of sudden tears.

He doesn't want me.

CHAPTER SIX

By the time the plane touched down in Las Vegas, Karen had experienced an epiphany. It had started when she'd left the lavatory and returned to the main compartment. Mason had moved across the cabin to sit beside Tristan, and as Karen went back to her seat, Tristan glanced in her direction, his brows narrowed, his face set in a murderously severe scowl.

He'd made no secret of the fact her presence displeased him, but up until that moment, she'd felt timid in response, as if she'd done something wrong and rightfully deserved his anger. With that look, that glower, something in her had snapped, and instead of looking away, she'd glared right back at him.

Fuck you, Tristan, she thought, hoping against hope his mind was open and he could hear her. *I'm tired of this, tired of the games—and of you.*

It might have been just her imagination, wishful thinking on her part, but she could have sworn that he looked away first, his expression growing somewhat sheepish, as if cowed by the ferocity in her stare.

By the time the jet touched down in Las Vegas—much to her white-knuckled relief—she found herself feeling considerably better, if not about flying, then about the status of her life. She had a three-step plan in mind, one she felt satisfied with.

Step one: call Michel as soon as we get to Las Vegas and give him my notice.

Step two: fall out of love with Tristan Morin—the sooner, the better.

Step three: enjoy my weekend.

A glossy limousine awaited them at the airport terminal—not one of the garish stretch varieties favored by teenagers on prom night, but a sleek, elegant sedan. The chrome wheel covers had each been emblazoned with *B*. Like his father, then, Karen observed, Mason preferred chauffeured Bentleys.

While Tristan lagged behind, Mason escorted her in genteel fashion, offering the crook of his elbow to guide her. As he swept her into the car and she settled back against the soft, buttery leather seats, she wondered vaguely why, if she had to be damned into a pair-bond attraction to one of the Brethren, it couldn't have been Mason instead.

As they drove down the legendary Las Vegas strip, she found herself staring childlike out the window at all the passing buildings and colorful signs.

"It's not as exciting as it is at night." From beside her, Mason sounded nearly apologetic, as if she should be disappointed in the view.

"Are you kidding?" She'd seen casinos before, of course—Reno was chock-full of them, as was the Nevada side of Lake Tahoe—but none of those compared. Craning her neck as they passed, she gawked at the towering black pyramid of the Luxor and the regal sphinx standing stoic guard in front of it. "This place is like Disneyland for grown-ups."

"This is the newer strip," Tristan said. "There's another one on Freemont Street, where a lot of the original casinos and hotels were built. They're connected beneath this enormous canopy structure, and after dark, they run light shows on the hour, all along the canopy underside."

These were the first words he'd said to her since they'd picked her up that morning, and she blinked at him, as dumbstruck as she'd been by the Luxor.

"Mason used to bring me along whenever one of his hotels here would open," Tristan continued, as if they hadn't spent the night before making love together, and as if after that he hadn't, for all intents and purposes, ripped her heart out of her chest, tossed it on the floor, and stomped on it a time or two for good measure. The fact that he sounded so nonchalant, so *normal,* suddenly infuriated her.

"One of my hotels," Mason repeated with a clumsy laugh, as if embarrassed. "You make it sound like I'm a mogul." Leaning into Karen's shoulder, he added, "I'm really more of a hobbyist."

"Not many 'hobbyists' have their own NASDAQ symbol," Tristan said, and Karen blinked again, this time in genuine surprise. "He's one of the principals at Triumvera Trust."

"Triumvirate," Mason corrected mildly. "It's a modest investment firm specializing in full-service and luxury hotels in the U.S. and abroad."

"With more than eight billion dollars in assets," Tristan added.

"Is the Trésor one of them?" Karen asked Mason, and when he nodded, she could have sworn he was blushing.

He'd shown her a picture of the resort on the plane, a conceptual rendering that had depicted a pair of towers that faced one another, with an expansive shopping plaza between them. He'd explained that several hotels would be housed within the nearly six-million-square-foot facility, as well as three permanent stage shows, eleven restaurants, six swimming pools, a conference center, and retail facilities.

In the painting, the towers had been shown at night, with gold-accented, cream-colored facades standing out in stark contrast to the dark sky. As they approached, Karen could see that in the bright, full light of the afternoon sun, however, the buildings gleamed like they'd been electroplated in gold, dazzling and stunning complements to the backdrop of mountains visible in the distance beyond the city's limits.

"Oh, Mason," she breathed, eyes wide, mouth agape. The top of the car had been fitted with a retractable moonroof, and with the press of a button, Mason had opened it so that she could crane her head back and gawk.

"You like it?" he asked, sounding hesitant, hopeful even, like a little boy showing a new toy to a playmate.

Tristan uttered a low whistle, and a sideways glance proved he was as visibly impressed as she felt. *"C'est magnifique,"* he said. *It's magnificent.*

Although Mason and Michel would sometimes lapse in and out of French with oblivious ease, Tristan seldom, if ever, followed suit. To hear him speak it now, with perfect dialect, raised the hairs along her nape, turning her on as instantly and powerfully as if he'd offered this within intimidate proximity of her ear. All at once the second step in her plan—*fall out of love with Tristan Morin*—so simple in the conception, seemed impossible.

Not if he keeps speaking French, at any rate, she thought.

****

The Trésor was indeed grand, even by the usually high standards of opulence an investment by Mason's trust

76

company demanded, enough so that even Tristan, who'd seen nearly every one of his uncle's properties, was dutifully impressed at the sight of it.

To that moment, his proximity to Karen, and the bloodlust this would usually provoke, had remained dormant in him, but all at once, he had a jolt of telepathic sensation from her. Like the bloodlust, his telepathy had been quiet and quelled during the trip to that point, and this sudden burst of awareness was fleeting but strong. It was the French that had done it, his speaking it aloud. She'd reacted to it, and in return, his body reacted to hers.

Fuck, he thought in bright, sudden alarm, because that was what he wanted to do—suddenly, urgently enough to feel an immediate, uncomfortable strain against the fly of his jeans when he looked at her. Her heart had raced, just for a moment in visceral, reflexive response to his voice, but it had been enough to send a cocktail of adrenaline and epinephrine surging through her.

Fuck, he thought again, because he could feel his gums tingling, a dim ache as his canine teeth inched forward. All at once, the dazzling glow of reflected sunlight off the tower facade seemed even more blinding—his pupils had begun to dilate.

The pills. He'd stuffed them into his traveling bag, which was now stowed away in the trunk of the Bentley.

"Here," he heard Mason say, then a quick snap of his seat belt as he unbuckled it. "Trade me sides." Reaching up, he pressed another button on the moonroof control panel, and the tinted glass retracted, letting in a rush of warm air. "You can stand up, look outside."

He wasn't speaking to Tristan, he realized dimly as he watched Karen likewise unfasten her own seat belt.

No, he thought, stricken, pressing himself back into his seat. *No, no, don't do that.*

Karen was oblivious, excited as she and Mason shifted positions, squirming to switch places on the seat bench. She'd taken off her coat at the airport, and when she stood, the hem of her sweater pulled up. Less than two feet away from him—well within biting distance—he could see a taunting glimpse of exposed skin at her lower back, and the upper edge of her panties.

Oh, Christ, he thought, clapping his hand to his mouth to muffle a groan. When he glanced at Mason, he found his uncle watching him with a bemused sort of expression, one brow slightly arched above the other.

Because he did it on purpose, Tristan realized. *If I could sense Karen's reaction, then he could too—and mine, along with it. You son of a bitch, Mason.*

The limousine jostled to an unexpected stop as they pulled into the valet area outside the resort. Karen lost her balance and stumbled sideways. Reacting out of instinct,

Tristan caught her, his hands shooting out, clamping against her hips. Her sweater was still askew, and his fingers touched her waist. Her skin was silken, soft and warm, and in that moment, he remembered the night before—taking her from behind, locking his fingers through hers, feeling helpless against her, helpless *without* her.

She blinked down at him, wide-eyed, and he blinked back, snapping out of his reverie. Could she notice his eyes, the slight descent of his teeth? God, he hoped not; his humiliation would be complete.

"I...I've got you," he said, his voice ragged and hoarse. He couldn't remove his hands from her. He tried not to think about how easy it would be to hook his fingertips beneath the waistband of her jeans and peel them down, her panties too—pull *her* down against him right there in the limo, in front of Mason, the driver, in front of God and everybody, because God, he didn't care.

"Uh...thanks," she said, sounding strained and uncertain.

"All right, *mes chéris.*" Mason clapped once, his mouth stretched in a delighted Cheshire Cat grin again as he reached for the door handle. "We've arrived."

CHAPTER SEVEN

"Let you get settled into your rooms a bit after check-in," Mason was saying, as their uniformed chauffeur, along with a scurrying bevy of bellhops and valets swarmed the vehicle, collecting the meager assortment of bags from the trunk of the Bentley. With a glance at his watch, he said, "It's shortly before five now. Why don't we plan to rendezvous in the main lobby by the main waterfall at six o'clock sharp?"

"The main waterfall?" Karen asked, blinking owlishly. "You mean there's more than one?"

"Oh yes, at least a dozen or so," Mason replied cheerfully. "And a river too." When her eyes widened all the more, he added, "It winds all through the resort complex, inside and out. You can take electric catamaran tours of it. I'll arrange one, if you'd like."

"I thought you said we weren't supposed to be at this party of yours until ten," Tristan said with a scowl.

Any good humor he might have managed—or Karen might have imagined—along the ride from the airport had abruptly faded. It had happened, she noticed, right about the time she'd nearly fallen into his lap while she'd stood to look out the sunroof. Tristan had caught her, helping to steady her without incident, but he'd been acting surly ever since, the proverbial cat that had been dunked in a toilet bowl.

Was it really so horrible for you to have to touch me? Funny. You didn't seem to mind it too badly last night.

"The soiree, no," Mason said. "But I've made arrangements that should keep us pretty well occupied in the meantime." He chuckled, then draped one arm around Tristan's shoulders, the other around Karen's, steering them both toward the entrance. Here, another cluster of uniformed staff waited to open doors in greeting. "Tell me, how does a warm stone massage, seaweed thermal body wrap, mint pedicure, organic chamomile compress, and facial sound?"

"I just buried my mother yesterday." Tristan hooked his bag from the bellhop's cart as it wheeled past. Shouldering his way past his uncle and Karen and tromping into the hotel, he added, "I doubt a bunch of seaweed's going to make any difference."

Karen had never heard Tristan speak so harshly to Mason before, and to judge by the way Mason sucked in a sharp, wounded breath, he hadn't either. He stopped in midstep, bringing Karen to a stumbling halt along with him while Tristan went on ahead.

"He had no right to say that," she said, because Mason looked like Tristan had just caught him with a sucker punch in the gut, leaving him breathless and dumbfounded and more than a little bruised. "In fact..."

Fuming, she shrugged away from Mason, meaning to follow Tristan into the hotel and confront him. *What the hell's your problem?* she wanted to demand, not just about how he'd spoken to his uncle, but about everything—the night before, that morning, the limousine ride just now.

"Let it go." Mason caught her by the hand.

"He had no right to say that," she said again, brows narrowed.

Mason smiled at her with more sorrow than humor. "Yes, he did."

****

Stepping foot into her suite was enough to make Karen forget her ire with Tristan, at least for a little while. Larger than her lakefront house back in Tahoe, the suite stood in elegant contrast to the glittering, somewhat garish skyline of the city beyond its windows. Freshly cut white roses and calla lilies had been arranged in vases throughout the suite, lending the room a sweet, delicate fragrance. The furnishings—cherry wood with alternating cornflower blue and cream-colored upholstery—were delicate and decorative, nearly Baroque in design. Lush drapes fell in sweeping ivory folds from the towering windows while the king-sized bed had been piled high with down-filled blankets and pillows, a skillfully arranged and wondrously inviting mountain of them.

"I hope it's to your liking, ma'am," the valet who had escorted her said as he walked ahead of her across the expansive breadth of the great room, snapping open drapes to let the waning afternoon sun spill across the floor.

"It's beautiful," she breathed, hating to feel like that stereotypical small-town girl from Kansas, all round eyes and agape as she looked around, but helpless to stop herself.

"This is our Queen Anne suite," the valet continued. "Many of the furnishings are authentic pieces from the early eighteenth century, when Anne of the House of Stuart served simultaneously as Queen of Britain, Ireland, and France."

She and Mason had parted company upon check-in. She'd lost track of Tristan at that point, although she'd still been pissed enough with him to not bother keeping much of an eye out for him anymore.

"About the party tonight..." Karen had said to Mason, with a gnawing anxiety in her voice. "You told me to pack lightly, so I did. I don't...I mean, I didn't bring anything to wear."

Not that she'd have had anything in her meager wardrobe, anyway. *A red-carpet event,* that's what Mason had called it. She'd seen enough awards programs and premiers on TV to understand what that meant.

"We have a shopping galleria here at the resort," Mason had told her with a reassuring smile.

But even with the generous salary Michel paid her, she doubted she'd be able to afford anything red-carpet worthy. Either this had been obvious in her crestfallen expression, or Mason had read her mind; either way, he'd chuckled and given her cheek a quick kiss.

"Don't worry," he'd said. "It's on me."

"But I...I..." she'd stammered, and he'd dropped a wink.

"Consider me your fairy godfather."

"Dr. Morin had a bottle of wine delivered already," the valet told her, and she followed his gaze to a small table where, beside an overflowing spray of white flowers, a bottle had been left uncorked to breathe. A pair of glasses flanked either side, and in front of it, a platter of colorful fresh fruits and sliced cheeses awaited.

"The wine is a 1996 Chateau Lafite-Rothschild Pauillac," the valet said as he went to the table and poured a dollop of the dark burgundy wine into the basin of one of the glasses. Swirling it gracefully, he presented it to her. "This Bordeaux vintage has been called 'the King's wine,' as it was once favored by Louis the Fifteenth of France. You'll find its texture silken, with lingering flavors of black currant and mint, with a strong tannin finish."

"Oh," she said, because she didn't know jack-shit about wine. Accepting the glass, she swished it around as she'd seen the valet do, then, because he continued watching her with a patient sort of expectation, she took a sip. "It's good."

"It costs an average of two thousand dollars a bottle," the valet told her helpfully, at which point, she nearly spit all over his crisply pressed slacks and well-polished shoes.

"It's very good," she amended weakly, once able to choke down a mouthful and speak. "Would you like a glass?"

The young man chuckled. "No, thank you, ma'am." He nodded once, politely, and when she fumbled to find some money to give him, a tip he wouldn't consider insulting, he'd shaken his head. "There's no need, ma'am. Dr. Morin has seen to all of the arrangements. Shall I return shortly before six to escort you to the lobby?"

"Yes," she said, nodding stupidly, still holding her wineglass. She had no idea what tannins were, but the kid had been right. The wine had a lingering aftertaste to it. She suspected it was called *money*. "Thank you. That...that would be nice."

When he'd left, she took a few moments to wander around the suite, staring in continued awe at the beauty of the room and all the elegant furnishings. Sinking onto the bed was like settling into a cloud; the mattress and bedding enveloped her, cradling her body, and she closed her eyes, releasing a long, heavy sigh. In that moment, it was all nearly worth it—the horrible, heartbreaking morning, the airplane flight from Reno, the bizarre and continuously tumultuous interactions with Tristan.

I could get used to this, she thought with a faint smile. But then, remembering her three-step plan, she forced herself to sit up, then return to the living room, where she fished her cell phone out of her travel bag.

To her immense relief, Michel's phone rang over to voice mail. Leaving a message would be so much easier, she told herself. *If I talk to him on the phone or try to tell him in person, he'll talk me out of it somehow. Not by using his telepathy or tricking me, but just by the way he is. I know it.*

Because that's exactly how she'd wound up working for him in the first place. After Tristan's two-year clinical rotation at the Sierra Nevada Medical Center had ended, he'd left and never returned. From Karen's perspective, at least at the time, it had been a good thing, because she'd been hard-pressed to get anything done whenever he'd been around. For almost two years after that, she'd gone about her nursing duties there, until one evening, halfway through a twelve-hour shift, a tall man in a camel-colored coat with striking green eyes had asked to speak with her.

There'd been something familiar, uncannily so, in his appearance, but it hadn't been until he'd introduced himself—Michel Morin—that she'd felt a shock of full, tremulous recognition.

Morin.

She hadn't realized at the time that Michel was Tristan's grandfather, because he hadn't introduced himself as such. There was no way she'd have believed him anyway, no way she could have fathomed how a man who barely looked old enough to be Tristan's father could be even older than this— much, much more so. Instead, Michel had told her he was a relative of Tristan's, and when he'd broached the subject of her possibly coming to work with Tristan at an exclusive medical clinic funded by the Pharmaceaux International research company, she'd been excited.

Had Tristan specifically recommended her? Had he remembered her after all that time? While to that point, they'd done nothing except work together in a completely professional, clinical setting, there had always been that undeniable, irresistible attraction to him—one she'd often felt certain he'd shared. The idea of seeing him again, working with him, being near him, had sent her heart racing with eager anticipation. The salary hadn't mattered; Michel could have offered her a pittance and she'd have accepted gladly.

Anything for Tristan, she thought in her Las Vegas suite with a frown. *That's how it's always been with me—anything for him. Well, not anymore.*

"Hey, Michel," she said, the note of good cheer in her voice not as forced as it might have otherwise been had she not just knocked back a glassful of the flavorful, ridiculously expensive wine Mason had bought her. "This is Karen. Listen, I really appreciate you letting me take some time off this weekend, but I have to tell you...I just don't think this is working out. It's been a year now, and I'm getting pretty homesick, and I've been thinking about just heading back east, back to Kansas for a while. I hate to leave you in a spot, but with things going so well lately with Eleanor's treatments, and with Lisette..." Her voice faltered as Tristan's words, angry and hurt, echoed in her mind.

I just buried my mother yesterday. I doubt a bunch of seaweed's going to make any difference.

"I just think it's best if I go," she finished in a rush, then thumbed off the phone to disconnect the call before she could say anything stupid, like try to take back her resignation. Idiotically, she found herself blinking against the dim heat of tears, and with a miserable little cry, she threw the phone across the room.

I couldn't live like this, she realized, looking around again, no longer seeing the room as something opulent, like out of a fairy tale, but rather imposing, like out of her league. *This isn't me. None of this is. This is Tristan's life, the Morins' life. Not mine.*

Less than an hour later, as Karen left her room in the company of the young valet, who had returned as promised, she paused in the corridor outside her door, her attention caught by the unexpected sound of piano music, something low and sorrowful and achingly familiar.

Tristan.

He and Mason both had suites on the same floor as hers; Mason's was directly across the hall, while Tristan's was further down. Mason was well acquainted with his nephew's remarkable musical talents and had obviously offered him accommodations with a piano to use as he pleased.

While the valet walked on ahead, oblivious to the sound, Karen turned, following the soft strains until they abruptly ended and she found herself outside suite number 1721—Tristan's. She knew the piece he had been performing: Beethoven's *Für Elise.* He'd often played it for his mother on the piano Michel had delivered to the clinic for this specific purpose, and had recorded it so that when he wasn't around, she could still hear its melancholy, haunting refrains. Lisette had been vegetative, nonresponsive at this point, with no discernable brain activity, but Tristan had been devoted nonetheless, as if through the song, he'd found some last semblance of physical and emotional connection to his dying mother.

In that moment, listening to the piano, Karen felt her heart ache for Tristan. She'd seen for herself, for more than a year, how fiercely dedicated he'd been to his mother's care, and he'd told her many times about how close he and Lisette had been. He'd felt protective of her, and in the end, responsible for her, and even though he'd likely come to terms with the grim reality of her impending demise years earlier, it couldn't have made the loss any less poignant or painful for him.

Oh, Tristan. She draped her hand lightly against his door—not a knock, but a caress, as if touching his face, offering him comfort. Closing her eyes, she leaned forward, pressing her forehead against the wood. *I know you're hurting. Why won't you let me help?*

After a moment, she had the strangest sensation—that Tristan had come to stand on the other side of the door, that he'd placed his hand against it just as she'd done, so that they were palm to palm, save for the panel of wood between them. She could swear that he, too, tucked his forehead against the door. He knew she was there, and he was torn inside. She could feel it somehow, feel *him*, and when he closed his eyes, she could see it in her mind; when he uttered a low, lonely sigh, she could hear it.

"I'm sorry," he whispered to her, and she heard him, plain as day, as if he'd offered this directly in her ear.

"Miss Pierce?" The valet's voice came from behind her, soft and hesitant, and she turned in surprise, eyes flying wide. "I'm sorry. I didn't mean to startle you."

Momentarily puzzled, if not somewhat disoriented, Karen looked back at Tristan's door. The sensation of him standing on the other side—if it had really been there at all—was now gone.

"Dr. Morin is waiting," the valet told her, sounding uncertain now.

She let her hand linger against the door for another moment, then drew away. Forcing a smile, she turned to the boy. "I'm sorry," she said. "Lead the way."

****

Tristan listened through the door as Karen walked away, her footsteps light on the carpet runner in the corridor outside. More than this, her fragrance faded with her, and he closed his eyes again, drawing in the last lingering hints of her sweetness from the air.

It had taken every ounce of strength he'd possessed not to open the door. Upon arriving at his suite, he'd promptly dug out the bottle of Wellbutrin from his bag and choked down another handful. His telepathy had been dampened along with any residual bloodlust again. He hadn't sensed Karen come to his door with his mind. Instead, it had been the scent of her body, so distinctive and appealing, that had drawn his attention away from his music.

"I'm sorry," he whispered again, wanting to throw open the door and race after her, catch her. *I didn't want to hurt you, Karen. Last night was amazing, but I fucked it all up. It's all my fault, and I'm sorry.*

Instead he retreated into the bathroom. Flicking on the bright, glaring overhead lights, he dug furiously through his small shaving kit until he found a razor. Working swiftly, he dismantled it, letting the double-edged stainless steel blade fall against the granite countertop. He took it in hand, then squatted on the floor, dropping to his knees in front of the toilet. Holding out his arms, he leveled them, bare and exposed, over the basin, and with his left hand, pressed the edge of the razor hard enough into the flesh just below his right wrist to leave a dent.

For a long moment, he sat there, poised and unmoving, his breath coming in short, ragged gasps. It wouldn't have taken much. The radial artery wasn't deep; even with the naked eye, he could see it pulsing beneath the delta of his thumb, marking the frantic, harried cadence of his heartbeat.

It could kill you.

Naima's voice and words came to mind, haunting him, making him hesitate. Two nights earlier, she'd said this to him. He'd come to her house shortly before midnight, wanting her to feed from him. Usually, she obliged him because to that point, she'd been in on his secret, his sick little fetish.

He liked to bleed.

Not just have a little blood drained from him, the scant amount needed to sustain the Brethren components of his or Naima's nature—Tristan liked to lose massive amounts of his blood, enough so that if he'd been human, he would die from hypervolemic shock. In fact, it was that state of reflexive physiological shock, an instinctive rush of endorphins through his veins, that made the experience so appealing to him. It was the ultimate high, his body's last desperate fight-or-flight reaction.

"No, Tristan." Naima had sat on her couch, her long legs tucked beneath her, her expression unreadable, unflappable. She'd watched him first unbutton, then shrug his way out of his shirt without saying a word, but when he'd stepped toward her, out of the shadows and into the dim circumference of light cast by a nearby lamp, she'd shaken her head. "Not tonight. Not ever again."

"What?" Bewildered, he'd blinked at her. She'd never denied him before. In fact, she'd admitted to him that a part of her—something primal and predatory in her nature—enjoyed the chance to physically overpower him, the way she imagined a cat must find a favorite toy stuffed with catnip particularly appealing. She'd drain him nearly dry, until that surge of epinephrine would course through him like a sexual climax, and he'd fall unconscious in its wake.

"It's not good for me," she said. "Michel thinks it may be causing some of the violent fugues I've been suffering. He said something about ingesting too much Brethren blood in one sitting causing a chemical imbalance in our brains. *Feral psychosis,* he called it." With a pointed glance, she added, "Not to mention, it could also kill you."

"You told Michel?" he'd asked in dismay. Although surely not the first Brethren to discover the elusive high that came with nearly bleeding to death, Tristan was the only one he knew who practiced the habit, and it was one he had no doubt his grandfather would disapprove of. "Great. Just great. That's the last fucking thing I need."

Humiliated, furious, he'd leaned down, snatching his shirt in hand.

Her brows had lifted, her face softening with gentle sympathy. "Tristan, Michel cares about you."

He'd managed a clumsy laugh. "Yeah."

"Why don't you believe that?"

She'd looked at him and he'd met her gaze, primarily because she'd forced him to through her telekinesis, enveloping his head in a firm but gentle bubble of energy and holding him fast, refusing to allow him to escape or avert his gaze.

Because he rules my life, he'd wanted to say. He'd wanted to shout it at her, hoarse and angry, his fists balled, his brows furrowed. *What I eat, what I drink, who I fuck, my job, my house, my car. He trapped my mom here, and now he's trapped me too. Or he thinks he has, at any rate. He doesn't care about me. He cares about controlling me, controlling my whole goddamn life. Because I'm not like you.*

I'm not like Mason or Rene or Brandon or anyone else. I'm a full-blooded Brethren, but a bastard son, and to Michel Morin, that's no better than being his bitch. His goddamn slave, Naima, and you of all people should know what that feels like!

He hadn't deliberately opened his mind to his sister and didn't know if she'd overheard him or not, but in the end, her face had hardened again, growing as smooth and cool as stone, and she'd let him leave without another word.

Tristan's brows furrowed as, in the bathroom of his hotel suite, he tried to summon some resolve and slash his wrist open. The bleeding would clear his mind. But even though he dug the edge of the blade deeper into his skin, he couldn't bring himself to do it.

It could kill you, he thought of Naima saying, and he let his fingers relax against the razor. With a soft *plunk,* it dropped into the toilet, sinking fast, winking with light reflecting off ripples above it.

She was right and he knew it. One of the reasons he didn't die when Naima bled him almost dry was because the coagulating enzymatic properties of her saliva prevented it. The Brethren could both naturally anesthetize their prey with their saliva, so that biting into them wouldn't hurt, but could also stave the flow of blood by accelerating the body's natural clotting mechanisms once their fangs had withdrawn. Within seconds after a Brethren released his or her bite from a victim, bleeding would all but cease.

95

With a razor blade, on the other hand, Tristan wouldn't have that kind of benefit. He could suck on his own wrist, of course, letting his own spit affect him, but there was always the chance that he'd pass out from blood loss before being able to do so sufficiently, if at all.

And in that case, I'd bleed out all over the floor. He thought of Karen finding him like that, or Mason. With a heavy sigh, he raked his fingers through his hair. *I can't do that to them.*

He heard a knock at his door and glanced over his shoulder. Although he opened his mind reflexively, the medication he'd taken had effectively muffled him, and as before, he could sense nothing discernible. Feeling strangely vulnerable because of this, he rose to his feet and went to the door, using the peephole to peer out into the corridor beyond.

"Mason." He opened the door, feeling sheepish and ashamed. "Look, about downstairs, what I said...how I acted earlier...I was out of line."

"Yes, you were," his uncle agreed with a nod. "But it's all right." With a gentle smile, he reached for Tristan. "I loved Lisette too."

He hooked his hand against the back of Tristan's neck and Tristan let him pull him against his shoulder in a kind embrace.

"I know," Tristan whispered, closing his eyes, feeling ridiculously close to tears. "I'm sorry."

"It's forgotten." Mason turned his head slightly, kissing Tristan fondly on the head through his hair. "Now put your shoes on and come with me."

As he drew back, Tristan shook his head. "Look, Mason. I appreciate the offer, that shit with the spa. Really. But..."

"But it's not your idea of a good time?" Mason asked.

"Not at all," Tristan admitted, and Mason laughed.

"I made the spa reservations for Karen," he said, clapping Tristan on the shoulder. "You and me—we've got a tee time to keep. How does that sound?"

Tristan wasn't much of a golfer either, but all at once, he didn't care. "Better than a seaweed wrap," he said, making his uncle laugh again.

CHAPTER EIGHT

Three hours later, Karen closed her eyes and uttered a long, contented sigh as she leaned back against the glass wall of the elevator. Her entire body felt liquefied, as if she'd been scraped hollow from head to toe and refilled with a thick, molten core of warm chocolate or butter.

"Are you all right, miss?" she heard a voice ask hesitantly, and she peeled back a reluctant eyelid, having forgotten she wasn't alone in the elevator car.

"I'm sorry," she said with a sheepish smile to the man riding with her. Her cheeks felt hot with sudden blush and she tried to laugh. "I'm fine. I just got finished at the Asiatique Spa, that's all."

"Oh." Brows raised in tandem, an *aha!* sort of expression, he nodded. "I'm more of a baccarat fan myself." Her puzzlement must have been apparent on her face, because he leaned toward her and, with a wink and another smile, added in a low, conspiratorial voice, "It's a card game."

"Oh." She laughed.

"It's a lot of fun," he promised. "I'd be glad to teach you if you have the time."

He said this last after a slight but discernable pause, his brow arched slightly to match the wry hook of his mouth.

I'll be damned, she thought, feeling bright new blush bloom in her cheeks. *He's hitting on me.*

The elevator shimmied slightly underfoot as it came to a stop. With a ding and a soft rumble, the doors parted.

"This is, uh, my floor," Karen said. "Thank you for the offer, though."

I'll be damned, she thought again, pressing her hand to her mouth to stifle giggles as she followed the corridor to her room. She'd been on her own at the resort's spa. When she'd arrived in the lobby at the impressive, multistory indoor waterfall and surrounding koi pond, she'd been greeted by a blonde woman in a formfitting *cheongsam*-style silk dress, who had introduced herself as Teá.

"Dr. Morin extends his apologies," Teá had told her with a smile. "As he will be unable to join us this afternoon."

"Us?" Karen had blinked stupidly, but Teá had continued to smile, offering her hand in invitation.

"Come with me, please, Miss Pierce," she'd said. "We have some wonderful treatments with which to lavish you today."

Lavish. Now there was the perfect word for it, Karen mused as she slipped her key card into the narrow slot in her front door and listened for the corresponding click. Any self-consciousness or awkwardness she'd felt once she'd stripped down and stepped into the room had dissolved the moment her masseuse draped his hands against her. Just about anything resembling conscious thought, for that matter, had dissolved at his expert touch, and from there, it had all been blissfully, wondrously downhill.

This may not be me, my life, but I could get used to it just the same, she thought as she crossed the front foyer of her suite, letting the door fall closed behind her. The sun was sinking low in the sky, and she had a nearly panoramic view of both the sunset beyond the mountains, and the neon glow of the strip as it came to life thirty-some-odd stories below.

To her surprise, she found several boxes on her bed, each fashioned with broad black satin bows. A card had been left atop the largest, the envelope unsealed, and when she pulled it out, she saw gilded Trésor stationary.

I hope you don't mind if I took a few liberties at the resort boutiques on your behalf, Mason had written inside, his script elegantly slanted, signed only with his initial, *M.*

Curious and excited, Karen untied the bow and let the ribbon droop in lank folds to the ivory bedspread. When she lifted the box top and gently pulled aside the thin layer of tissue paper inside, she uttered a soft gasp.

Oh my God.

It was gorgeous—a black silk halter dress with straps that fastened behind the neck and a hem that hit her at midthigh when she held it up beneath her chin. The empire waist had been fitted with elegant gathers, while the skirt flowed with a flirty buoyancy. The label read *Badgley Mischka,* the price tag, $650.

"Oh my God."

In the smaller box, she found a pair of shoes, black satin stilettos with a price of $200.

"Oh my God," she whispered again, and this time, a laugh escaped.

She heard a knock at the door to her suite, and when she turned, saw another small envelope whisk suddenly beneath, pushed through from the hallway. Intrigued, she set the shoes aside and went to retrieve it—another note from Mason on a second Trésor letterhead card: *A few more liberties.*

She squinted through the peephole, then drew back in surprise to find four young women waiting patiently in the corridor just outside, each carrying several large, cumbersome cases.

"May I help you?" Karen asked, opening the door, bewildered.

"Dr. Morin sent us, Miss Pierce," said one of the women with a bright, enthusiastic smile.

"Wh-what for?" she stammered, at a loss.

"I'm from the Cartier pavilion downstairs," said a redhead dressed in a smart black pantsuit, carrying what looked like a locked briefcase.

"Cartier?" Karen blinked. "You mean, like the jewelry store?"

"I'm from Petite Coquette, our in-house lingerie boutique," said another.

"And we're from the resort salon," said the last, indicating the girl standing beside her. "My name is Andi. We'll be doing your hair and makeup for this evening."

"Hair and makeup?"

Andi's smile remained patient and bright. "Yes, ma'am. We can get started just as soon as you let us in."

Karen blinked as if she'd been pinched, realizing that she'd been standing in her doorway like an oak tree, immobilized and gawking. Blushing, she drew back, managing a laugh. "Of course. Please come in. I'm sorry."

"No need to apologize." Still beaming, Andi and the other women strode briskly past her, trundling their cases and bags into the suite. "It's our pleasure, Miss Pierce."

****

"My God, you have a beautiful swing," Mason remarked as Tristan brought his four-iron around in graceful follow-through after a hearty approach shot on the final green. To the man sitting next to him in the golf cart, he said, "Look at him. Back arched, hips squared, feet perfectly planted. It's like Michelangelo sculpted him."

"Beautiful," the other man, Jaime, agreed with a nod. Once upon a time, Mason might have introduced him to Tristan as "Uncle" Jaime.

Then again, maybe not, Tristan thought. Those Mason had dubbed "uncles" in Tristan's youth had been men with whom he'd been romantically involved for several months, sometimes years. There hadn't been a person like that in Mason's life for a long time, at least three or four years. Jaime was obviously someone Mason had met before, as he'd been waiting for them upon their arrival at the golf course, and Mason liked him well enough to bother introducing him to Tristan—as close to a nod of acknowledgment or approval from his family as he would seek or receive—but even so, they'd done little together except share a bench in the golf cart. It had also been Tristan's uncomfortable observation that Jaime's eyes had been riveted with unflinching interest on *his* ass, not Mason's, throughout the duration of their game.

When Tristan turned, walking back to the cart, he didn't miss the way Jaime's eyes cut up from that general vicinity to fix on his face, the corner of his mouth curling up in a wry sort of smile. "Just beautiful," he murmured again.

"It's getting dark." Forcing a smile, Tristan shoved his club back into the bag. "How about we call it a game?"

Let's get the hell back to the hotel, he wanted to add but bit back.

Mason looked puzzled. "We haven't played through yet."

"I'm at what? Ninety-two?" Tristan asked, fighting the urge to either cover his crotch with his hands or punch Jaime in the nose, because he could feel the other man's gaze crawling along his torso, working its way south. "You're eighty."

Mason looked down at the score card, then squinted to read his handwriting in the fading daylight. "Eighty-three. Jaime's around a hundred." He cut a glance at Jaime. "You really suck at this."

"And a lot of other things," Jaime replied, and they both laughed out loud. He was by far more flaming than any of Mason's former companions that Tristan had ever met, that was for sure. And he brought out in Mason a degree of flamboyance that Tristan was wholly unaccustomed to, if not somewhat unnerved by.

"Okay, then," he said loudly enough to interrupt. "Didn't you say we had dinner reservations at eight?"

"Eight-thirty," Mason said, and when Jaime looked wounded—obviously not invited—he patted him kindly on the leg. "Here, now. I'll join you later for cocktails in the penthouse lounge. How does that sound?"

Back at the resort, feeling surly, if not somewhat violated, Tristan tromped ahead of his uncle to the elevators.

"What did you think of Jaime?" Mason asked, cheerfully oblivious on the way up to their floor.

Tristan arched his brow. "He kept checking out my ass."

"And well he should," Mason replied primly, "as he has exemplary taste in these things."

"What the hell are you doing with a guy like that?" Tristan asked.

"Like what?" Mason said. "Oh, come on now. I know he may seem a little over the top..."

"A little?"

"But he makes me feel young again," Mason said.

Tristan folded his arms. "You were never *not* young to being with."

The elevator chimed just as Mason opened his mouth to reply. The doors rumbled open, and Tristan was instantly aware of a tingling sensation, light and electrical inside of his mind, raising the hairs against the nape of his neck. Mason obviously felt it too, because his smile abruptly faltered.

Someone's out there, Tristan realized. *Someone like us.*

A group of young women, all dressed in glittering, sequined cocktail dresses and high-heeled shoes, pushed aboard, giggling together, conflicting scents of their perfumes filling in the elevator cab in a sudden, suffocating cloud. Laughing together, jockeying for space, and teetering on their stilettos, they bumped into Tristan, making him stumble sideways and avert his gaze before he could get a clear look beyond them. When he glanced back, the doors had just slid closed again, and the elevator was underway.

"Oh no," one of the women lamented. "We're going *up!*"

They all moaned together, but Tristan ignored them, looking toward his uncle, all at once damning the side effects of the Wellbutrin that had dimmed his telepathic abilities to nonexistent.

"Did you sense that?" Once he and Mason had stepped off the elevator on their floor, Tristan caught him by the sleeve.

"Yes," Mason said grimly. "Someone must have bathed in Chanel No. 5." With melodramatic gestures, he flapped the front of his shirt, as if airing it out. "A little goes a long way with the classics, *mes chéris,*" he called to the closed elevator doors, the girls who were now long gone.

"What?" Tristan frowned, then chased after him, hooking him by the arm again as he started to walk away. "No, I mean back there. On the eleventh floor." He blinked at his uncle in visible bewilderment. "You didn't sense another one of us?"

Mason chuckled. "That's not possible. There are no other Brethren here."

"But I felt it," Tristan protested.

"You were sensing me. Sometimes, in a crowd of humans, our awareness of each other is momentarily heightened. Especially with overwhelming sensory input—like that perfume—to stimulate us."

That's not it, Tristan thought. *That's not what happened.*

"What about that Davenant guy, Jean Luc, you said Naima and Michel fought with last night in the woods?" he pressed. "What if it's him or someone else from their family?"

Mason looked at him for a long moment, then smiled. "Tristan," he said gently. "The odds of Jean Luc Davenant following us all of the way from Lake Tahoe to Las Vegas—with us airbound, no less—would be one in ten thousand. At least. And the odds of another Davenant stumbling upon us at this exact resort on this exact date are probably closer to one in a million."

"But..." Tristan began.

Mason pressed his fingertips against his mouth. "I'm sorry Jaime upset you," he said quietly, his brows lifting, his eyes mournful. "I shouldn't have invited him along. He didn't mean any harm, but I know he can seem a bit...uninhibited."

"That's not..." Tristan said, but Mason shook his head.

"Listen to me," he said in a low but firm voice. "There are no other Brethren here. I would never, ever risk putting you or Karen in harm's way. I promise."

As his hand slipped away, Tristan managed a scowl. "I can handle myself, Mason. I'm not a child."

"Yes, but you're the closest I've got," Mason replied, smiling again. "And I love you, silly boy. So humor me anyway and let it lie. We'll be late for dinner otherwise."

CHAPTER NINE

Consider me your fairy godfather.

Truer words had never been spoken, Karen figured, as she stood in front of the floor-length mirror in her room, marveling at her reflection. *Because I sure feel like Cinderella right about now.*

The necklace she'd selected was simple yet lovely, a slim filigree chain of white gold adorned with a modest scattering of diamond-encrusted rosettes. She'd deliberately chosen the least opulent piece from among the resort's proffered selection but had still nearly choked when she'd found out the price—forty-six thousand dollars.

"Holy shit," Karen had said, her stomach twisting into an anxious knot. "He—Dr. Morin can't possibly mean for me to keep this."

"Oh no," the young woman from Cartier had told her with a reassuring smile. "It's on loan for the night at his personal request." Because she must have seen the apprehension still obvious in Karen's eyes, she'd added, "It's fully insured. Catherine Zeta-Jones wore this very same piece last season to the Oscars."

"Holy shit."

The shoes fit her perfectly, as did the dress, and beneath, she wore the prettiest—although skimpiest—black satin bustier, panties, and garter belt she'd ever seen. The stylists had touched up the highlights in her hair to give her a sun-kissed look, while her makeup was expertly applied, with dusky shades around her eyes and crimson on her lips.

"I feel like a princess," she'd whispered before the women had left, blinking at herself in stupefied amazement, her eyes brimming with tears.

"You look like a goddess," Andi had replied, giving her hair one final fluff and spray. Laughing, she'd leaned in to buss Karen's cheek. "Don't cry now. You'll muss your mascara. And you'll make us cry too."

Mason had left word that he would come to get her at quarter past eight, for dinner reservations at eight thirty. It was now almost ten after, and she'd been alone for the better part of twenty minutes, pacing restlessly back and forth, letting her feet adjust to the new shoes and the unfamiliar height of the spindly heels.

At a knock on her door, she hurried to answer, grinning broadly, excited to show Mason his handiwork. To her surprise, when she swung the door open wide, she found a

young concierge holding a long white box between his
hands.

"Miss Pierce?" he asked, and when she nodded,
dumbfounded, he offered the box to her. Inside, she heard
something rustle slightly, the contents shifting. "These are
for you."

"Me?" Lifting the lid, she saw green tissue inside and
caught a fragrant whiff of roses. A dozen perfectly formed
blooms rested in a nest of green paper, their long, spindly
stems bound together with a satin bow. "How beautiful."
She gasped, looking up at the concierge. "Who are they
from?"

She wondered if Mason had sent them, or—with a thrill
of excitement and hope—Tristan.

"They're compliments of Mr. David Donnelly," the
concierge said. Obviously, he'd expected this name to have
some meaning to her, because when she simply blinked at
him, still at a loss, his bright smile faltered. "Mr. Donnelly is
our guest for the grand-opening gala this evening. He owns
one of the largest enterprise software companies in the world
and designed the resort's reservation system. He said you
met earlier. After your spa visit."

"Oh!" Her eyes flew wide in realization as she
remembered the man on the elevator.

"Mr. Donnelly said that he hopes you'll consider his
earlier offer standing," the concierge said.

I'm more of a baccarat fan myself. I'd be glad to teach you if you have the time.

"That, uh, that's very nice of him," she stammered.

"Yes, ma'am." The valet nodded once.

"Uh, okay then. Thank you." Stepping quickly back, Karen slammed the door shut. She clutched the box of roses for a long, bewildered moment. She didn't know if the concierge had expected her to offer some sort of reply through him—like something out of a romantic comedy movie—and peeked once through the spy hole to make sure he'd left.

What could I say? she thought, carrying the roses to the bedroom. *Please tell Mr. Donnelly that Miss Pierce says thank you for the flowers. She'd really like to take him up on his invitation, since he's probably a multi-gazillionaire and all, but she's currently rebounding from a one-night stand with a vampire. One impossible relationship at a time, please.*

She burst out laughing.

Another knock at the door, and this time, when she opened it, Mason stood waiting for her. Immaculately dressed in a crisp tailored suit, his dark hair swept back from his brow, he smiled to see her, his brows raising appreciatively as his gaze swept down the length of her form.

"What do you think?" she asked, nervous but eager, blushing brightly as she glanced down at herself.

"Beautiful," she heard someone say, but it wasn't Mason, and she looked up in surprise to find Tristan standing behind his uncle, his eyes enormous, fixed on her.

The heat in her cheeks blazed even more brightly as his attention remained riveted, unflinching and marveling. He looked startled—no, better yet, *stunned*—as if the idea of her cleaning up so well had never occurred to him, or as if he saw her—*really* saw her—for the first time.

"You look beautiful," he whispered at length.

"Thank you, Tristan," she whispered back, blushing all the more. If the truth be told, he looked pretty amazing himself—a charcoal gray jacket worn open over a darker gray shirt and slacks, everything tailored perfectly to fit his tall, lean form. He'd showered and shaved, combed his hair, applied a hint of cologne, something spicy and faint but pleasantly discernable. The flowers on her bed, and the man who'd sent them, were all but forgotten.

"Are you hungry?" Mason asked as she continued staring at Tristan, seized with the thought that if she were to catch him by the front of his shirt and pull him in stumbling tow across her threshold, she doubted he'd protest. The look in his eyes had shifted from surprise to appreciation and then to something else more visceral and needful.

She wanted to steel herself against him, against *wanting* him in return, to remind herself of how callously he'd treated her all day, how coldly he'd been toward Mason upon their arrival. She wanted to think, *Fuck you, Tristan*—more than anything, she wanted to laugh in his face and tell him, *You had your chance. You blew it, pal.*

But she kept thinking of the strains of *Für Elise* she'd heard from his room, and that uncanny sensation that he'd come to stand opposite her at his door, his heart aching as badly as her own.

"Karen?" With a bemused smile, Mason cocked his head to glean her attention.

Laughing, she forced herself to look away from Tristan. "I'm sorry. What? Hungry, yes. I'm starving."

And considering she was wearing a loaner necklace that netted forty grand retail, thanks to him, she had no doubt that dinner would be nothing less than spectacular.

She was right.

The restaurant looked more like a nightclub than anything else, with contemporary furnishings trimmed in neon and chrome. Seating arrangements were separated from each other into cozy, semiprivate alcoves by floor-to-ceiling panels of frosted glass between which water flowed in rippling, shimmering, multicolored falls. Beneath these, the floor was translucent, and the water continued to surge in winding, illuminated paths beneath patrons' feet and seats.

The décor may have been modern, but the fare was classic. After settling into their seats in a far corner of the main dining area, their meal kicked off with appetizers—*foie gras* with walnut nougatine, truffle crème anglaise and perigord black truffle; short ribs with roasted cauliflower, five-spice applesauce and a nutmeg-hazelnut froth, and braised ostrich with empanada, ceviche, black-bean puree, and green coconut rice. For her entrée, Karen indulged in herb-crusted Norwegian salmon, confetti pearl barley, and parsley coulis. Each dish was paired with generous servings of complementary wines.

Most amazing was the fact that Tristan actually *spoke* to her again, as if the night before and the wretched morning that followed had never happened and everything was the way it had used to be between them—friendly and fun, relaxed and unforced. The wine, like the food, was rich and abundant, and by the time they reached the dessert—warm chocolate fondant with almond-mocha ice cream and amaretto caramel—they were all tipsy and jovial, laughing together.

"You wouldn't last a day as a human," Mason told Tristan with a broad grin as he tossed back the latest in a seemingly endless line of glasses of wine.

"What?" Tristan laughed.

"You wouldn't know what to do with yourself if you couldn't use your telekinesis or telepathy," Mason said. "That's the problem with Michel keeping you and Naima cooped up at that compound. You forget there are more things in heaven and earth than are dreamt of in your

Brethren philosophies, to paraphrase the Bard. Look at me. Do you think I use my telepathy day in and day out with the kind of reckless—not to mention impolite—abandon your sister employs? Better yet, can you imagine the reaction I'd get in my operating suite if I starting tossing scalpels or forceps around using only my mind, like you? To be able to survive in the human world, we should appreciate what it means to *be* human."

"I *do* appreciate it," Tristan said, and Mason glanced at Karen dubiously, then laughed. "I do. I know what it's like to be around humans on a regular basis. I've been working for more than a year now at a human clinic in Reno." When both Karen and Mason turned to him in surprise, he settled back in his seat, folded his arms across his chest, and nodded once. "That's right."

"When?" Karen asked, because to the best of her knowledge, she and Tristan shared long shifts at the Lake Tahoe clinic, with him picking up most of the overnight hours, at least while Lisette had required around-the-clock care.

"At least three times a week. I pick up days there, so it doesn't interfere with work at the compound."

"Does Michel know?" she asked.

"Are you kidding?" It was Tristan's turn to laugh. "I'm still alive, aren't I?"

"You have a point." Undue though it seemed at times from her perspective as an impartial observer, Michel had always been harder on Tristan than his other children or grandchildren when it came to independence and freedoms beyond the compound. She'd always thought it was due to Tristan's relative youth and inexperience.

"I can handle an entire day as a human," Tristan continued, speaking to Mason, lifting his wineglass in hand as if either offering a toast or extending a challenge, a friendly sort of wager. "No problem."

"No powers," Mason reminded with a wry smile.

"No problem," Tristan said again. "Brandon Noble lived that way for years. And I've done it myself—today, in fact."

"*Quoi?*" Mason's good humor shifted to genuine surprise. *What?*

"Brandon told me about this crazy idea he had while he was living in Kentucky, to stop the bloodlust in him. He used medication to do it—buproprion."

"You mean Wellbutrin?" Karen asked, puzzled. "But that's an antidepressant."

"A unique kind of antidepressant," Mason remarked, looking thoughtful. "One of few that act primarily on dopamine, a neurotransmitter, in the brain. Michel's conducted tests that indicate spikes in our dopamine levels when we feed. Dopamine triggers the pleasure centers in our brains. It feels good when it's released—like during sex too—so we inherently seek to repeat those behaviors and activities that produce it. That's why the bloodlust is so difficult to resist. The bupropion prevents the reuptake of dopamine in nerve endings, which decreases its effect and its influence on the brain." Raising his brows, visibly impressed, he said, "Brandon Noble came up this?"

"He stumbled on it by accident," Tristan replied. "But he told me it worked. I think it also must have side effects he was unaware of, though—the dampening of his powers. He told me he had trouble using telepathy when he lived in Kentucky. At the time, I assumed it was because Augustus was blocking him."

"Why don't you think so now?" Karen asked.

"Because I tried it myself," Tristan said. "Today. I took a massive dose to get it to therapeutic levels in my system. And I haven't been able to use my telepathy or telekinesis ever since."

Mason's eyes flew wide. "Have you lost your mind?" he exclaimed.

Tristan laughed. "Not that I'm aware of."

"Why would you do something like that?" Karen asked. "You don't know what kind of effect putting that much into you could have on your body."

"I'm fine." He awarded her a smile that she might have ordinarily been charmed by, but at the moment, she was preoccupied by marveling at how incredibly asinine he'd been.

"Except your powers don't work," she said drily.

"Yeah. I'm basically human. And yet somehow I've survived." Tristan directed this last with a pointed look at his uncle. Then, scooting his chair back from the table, he started to rise. "Excuse me a moment. I'll be right back."

He walked away from the table, pausing only long enough to direct the server with a quick nod to refill their wineglasses.

"He's crazy," Karen said with a frown. "He could've suffered seizures, muscle spasms, tardive dyskinesia..."

"Do you want to know why he did it?" Mason interjected softly, little more than a murmur.

She turned to him and he chuckled. "To be around you."

"What are you talking about?"

Mason smiled. "I told you on the plane. You're his pair-bond. But he's afraid of what that means, or rather, what yielding to his bloodlust and feeding from you would mean."

She shook her head. "I don't understand. What would it mean?"

Except that we were meant to be together, she thought.

"That Michel was right," Mason replied. "And as you're probably well aware, the boy would rather scrape out his own eye with a soup spoon than admit that possibility."

Leaning across the table toward her, he said in a low voice, "Has it ever occurred to you that it was more than just a coincidence how Michel tracked you down, offered you the clinic job?"

Karen shook her head. "What are you talking about? Tristan told him about me. That's what Michel said. He remembered me from his oncology residency in Reno and recommended me."

Mason shook his head, and she felt a sudden sinking feeling in the pit of her gut. She'd *never* seen Tristan and Michel have much by way of a civil conversation together. The interactions between the two had historically been tension filled and strained. *So why did I think they might have sat around and shot the shit one day about hiring a human nurse, that my name just casually popped up along the way?*

It made such sense to her in that instant, she wondered why in the hell she'd ever believed otherwise.

"Tristan believes that Michel brought you to the clinic to try to force the pair-bonding between you."

"And did he?" she whispered in dismay.

"I don't know." Mason tipped his head back, swallowing the last of his port. "I'm not my father. I've always thought that Michel brought you among us to try to make him happy. But Tristan has long held this ridiculous notion that Michel hates him, that he's hell-bent not just on controlling his life, but ruining it as well. I can't imagine Michel wanting that for anybody, least of all his own blood kin." With a gentle smile, he said, "But Tristan is very young yet, and naive. Not to mention stubborn as hell."

He stood, reaching beneath the lapel of his jacket for his cigarette case. "If you'll excuse me, I feel the need for a spot of air and a smoke. I'll be back in a moment." He leaned over, kissing her cheek. "Don't give up on the boy," he whispered, his voice unexpectedly ragged, a hoarse, mournful plea. "He can't fight what's in his nature forever. Or his heart."

****

I shouldn't have told them about the clinic job.

In the men's room, Tristan leaned over the marble sink basin, cupped his hands beneath the cold-water tap, and splashed his face. Sputtering, he shook his head once, then doused himself again. Blinking blindly against water droplets caught in his eyelashes, he looked up into the mirror just as the bathroom valet offered him a white terrycloth hand towel with which to mop himself dry.

"Thank you," Tristan croaked, his voice muffled as he buried his face into it.

"My pleasure, sir," the valet replied.

Even if they don't say anything to Michel about it, it's going to be in their minds. He'll find out by reading their thoughts, whether they want him to or not.

As if that wasn't stressful enough for him to consider, there was also the matter of Karen's legs to weigh on his mind.

Goddamn it, why does she have to be wearing garters?

For the better part of the last hour, Tristan had been stealing sideways glances beneath the edge of the white linen tablecloth, admiring the unintentional view of Karen's thigh—or more specifically, the black satin strap of her garter and the uppermost band of her stockings—as tantalizingly revealed by the drape of her skirt.

Nothing turned him on harder or faster than a woman in garters. That had long been his Achilles' heel, his absolute weakness. *And Mason knows it too,* he thought, lowering the towel so he could again peer at his reflection in the mirror above the sink. *Which is, I'm sure, exactly why he bought them for her.*

His hair was now damp and askew. He tried to rake it back into place with his fingers, and grimaced at the results. Wordlessly, the valet stepped to the rescue again, offering him a comb that had, to that point, been floating in a large jar of blue Barbicide solution.

"Thanks." Feeling sheepish, Tristan accepted it.

The valet nodded demurely. "My pleasure, sir," he said again.

He'd let it slip about his work at the Reno clinic in part because the wine had loosened his tongue, but also because he'd been completely floored by how amazing Karen looked. She was a beautiful woman; of that, he'd never had any doubt. But that night was different; that night, she was practically aglow. Her eyes, skin, hair, smile—all of it radiant and mesmerizing. He'd been floored at the sight of her, damn near struck speechless for likely the first time in his entire life.

And the garters.

Closing his eyes, he pinched the bridge of his nose and let out a long, slow sigh. At the sight of those straps, all sorts of ideas had played in his mind, images of the two of them from the night before, memories of what it had felt like inside her—hot, wet, wondrous—of how she'd sounded, how she'd tightened against him when she'd climaxed. Just the idea of easing her dress skirt slowly up, exploring the origins of those slim black satin ribbons laying tautly flush against her thighs had left him sporting a hard-on insistent enough to be painful.

But it's more than that.

He opened his eyes and blinked in surprise to find the valet offering him a packet of ibuprofen in one hand, a sample of Excedrin in the other.

"No, thanks," he said, managing a smile. "I'm good."

The valet nodded again. "As you wish, sir."

Do you honestly expect me to believe that the two of you never interacted except to care for Lisette? Mason had asked him of Karen on the flight from Reno. *You never talk to her? Never ask about the weather, offer to buy her a cup of coffee, for God's sake?*

The truth was, while working together, Tristan and Karen *had* talked. Long and often. On more than one occasion, he'd found himself sharing things with her that he'd never confided to anyone else. He'd talked to her about his mother, his helpless grief at her illness and his inability to offer more to her than palliative care. He'd talked to her about Michel and the tumultuous, antagonistic relationship the two of them shared. He'd told her of his hopes, dreams, and aspirations for a future beyond the compound—away from Michel.

He'd shared a lot of these same things with Tessa Noble one week earlier, because he'd been desperate for a connection with her, but it had been a forced bond between them, one born out of despondency on both of their parts over things that they could not influence or control.

You don't want this, she'd said to him as they'd stood together at the quickie wedding chapel in Reno, preparing to elope. He'd been filling out a marriage license application, when she'd touched his hand, stopping him. *Your heart isn't in this. It's miles away, back in Lake Tahoe. Just like mine.*

He and Karen had talked that night over dinner just as they always had, just as he'd always loved, when he could bullshit himself into thinking that it was because the clinical setting kept his bloodlust at bay, kept him from wanting her. The truth was, it hadn't. He could see that clearly now. It hadn't kept protected him from her at all.

Because I fell in love with her. And I'm still in love with her now. Last night had nothing to do with the bloodlust, nothing to do with grief. It was all about me, my feelings for her, things I've hidden away and denied for too long.

"I'm in love with Karen," he said softly.

The valet, having overheard this, quickly stepped forward again, a foil-wrapped condom in one hand, a peppermint in the other.

"No, thanks," Tristan said again, and this time his smile was less forced. He felt like he'd just hefted a massive weight from his shoulders with the quiet admittance. Now there was only one thing left to do.

I have to tell her how I feel. I have to tell her the truth.

"As you wish, sir," the valet said, walking away, returning the candy and condom to individual baskets on his countertop service tray. Tristan dropped a fifty-dollar bill into his tip jar on his way out of the room, and the valet gawked at the sight of it, clearly flabbergasted. "Thank you, sir," he exclaimed.

Reaching for the door, Tristan dropped him a wink. "My pleasure."

Then he frowned, as he noticed the same statically charged sensation tingling his skin that he'd felt earlier that day in the elevator. It came almost directly from the other side of the door.

Mason, he thought with a wry smirk. *Probably coming to try to trick me into escorting Karen back to her room in the hopes we'll hook up on the way.*

"You're too late," he said, pushing the door open, his mouth already stretching into a grin. "I've already decided to do this my way and..."

His voice faltered, and he blinked in bewildered surprise at the empty foyer outside the door. There was no sign of Mason; only a man at a nearby wi-fi hot spot with his laptop in hand, a pair of girls in cocktail gowns checking voice mail messages on their cells, and an older woman making her way from the main dining area to the lavatory.

That's weird, he thought, walking down the corridor until it dead-ended roughly twenty feet down the line. Backtracking, he followed it the other way, peering around columns and corners. Still no sign of his uncle.

With a frown, he returned to the restrooms, and once again, that uncanny, crawling sensation returned, so strong now, it left him flinching reflexively, cutting his eyes this way and that, his brows narrowed.

What the fuck is going on? Again, he damned himself for taking so many of the Wellbutrin, because he couldn't open his mind and better scan his surroundings, the psyches of anyone in his immediate vicinity.

Tristan.

He heard a man's voice, low, nearly a purr, resonate in his mind. Whirling, wide-eyed and startled, he looked behind him, but there was no one except the man with the laptop, who noticed his sudden, harried movement and glanced at him, momentarily curious.

That's your name, isn't it, poppet? It's a lovely one too.

Again, Tristan whirled, stumbling in surprise.

Just like you are, he heard this unfamiliar voice croon. *Quite lovely.*

Who the hell is this? Tristan's brows furrowed and he closed his hands into fists. He couldn't actively project his thoughts with his telepathy out of commission, but if the son of a bitch was already in his head, he'd be privy to it nonetheless. *Where are you?*

How handsome you look in your brand-new suit. It fits you well. You're...what? Six-one? Six-two? Maybe one hundred seventy-five pounds?

Where are you hiding? Tristan turned in a circle, scanning everything and everyone, searching. He was close by, then, whoever was taunting him, near enough to get a good look at Tristan, to size him up. *Come out and face me, you chickenshit son of a bitch.*

And that cologne you're wearing... Inside Tristan's mind, the man made an exaggerated sniffing sound that made him cringe reflexively, shrugging as if someone had just breathed too closely to his ear uninvited. *Ah. Armani Code. Very nice.*

Show yourself! Tristan snapped, his knuckles blanching white from the force with which he clenched his fists. In his mind, he heard a quiet chuckle but nothing else. Spinning in another frantic, clumsy O, he stared all around him. The man with the computer got up and walked toward the bathroom, tucking the laptop beneath his arm. The cell-phone girls noticed his anxious attention and looked away, whispering to each other and shooting suspicious glances in his direction. The matronly woman walked briskly away from the ladies room, a scrap of toilet paper caught in her shoe heel trailing behind her.

Goddamn it, answer me, Tristan snapped in his mind, but there was no response. The tingling sensation of another Brethren close at hand began to fade. As it did, a new thought occurred to him, one that left his heart shuddering in bright, new, and sudden alarm.

They think he'd been hiding out for at least a day in the woods near her house, Mason had warned him of Jean Luc Davenant and his potential interest in Karen.

"Shit." Tristan gasped, darting for the restaurant again, nearly crashing into a waitress carrying a tray filled with drinks along the way. *Karen!*

CHAPTER TEN

Karen sat alone at the table, cradling what remained of her glass of port in her hand.

Don't give up on the boy. Mason's words kept turning over inside her mind, over and over. *He can't fight what's in his nature forever. Or his heart.*

Could he be right? she wondered. *But why would Tristan want to fight it if it's something he really feels, like Mason said?*

"Where's Mason?" Tristan came rushing back to the table, shoving his way past a waitress.

"Outside," Karen said, confused and more than a little alarmed by his appearance. Gone was the relaxed young man who had sat beside her less than fifteen minutes earlier. He looked out of breath, as if he'd sprinted all the way back from the restroom, his eyes wide, his face ashen, his forehead glistening with a light sheen of anxious perspiration. "He went to smoke a cigarette." Hesitant to ask but unwilling not to, she ventured, "Is something wrong?"

"Yes." Marching smartly toward her, Tristan caught her by the wrist, yanking her forcibly to her feet. Surprised, she tottered unsteadily on her tiptoes for a moment, then yelped as he hauled her in stumbling tow for the front of the restaurant.

"What is it?" she asked, and when he didn't answer, she frowned. Planting her stilettos, she tried to shrug away from his grasp. "Tristan, stop. What's going on?"

"Leaving so soon, *mon lapin*?" All smiles as he returned, Mason nearly plowed into them headlong.

"We're *all* leaving," Tristan replied sharply, grabbing his uncle by the sleeve and spinning him around. When next he spoke, it was through gritted teeth, his voice deliberately low, but Karen was close enough to overhear. "You were wrong. There *is* someone here, another Brethren."

"What?" Karen gasped, her eyes flying wide.

"I told you earlier..." Mason began, his smile fading, his expression growing stern.

"I know what you told me, and I'm telling you now—*you were wrong.* He's here. I don't know how he found us, but he did. I heard him in my head. He knows my goddamn name, Mason."

"Who?" Karen asked, and when neither of them men averted their gaze from each other and acknowledged nor answered her, she frowned. "Who? You said another

Brethren. Is it the one Michel and Naima found in the woods, the Davenant?"

At first, she didn't think she'd get a response. The three of them stood in a tight cluster for a moment. Then, with a heavy sigh as he pushed his fingers through the heavy crown of his dark hair, Mason said quietly, "Yes, *ma chérie*. I believe there's a very strong likelihood that it's him, indeed. His name is Jean Luc."

"Why would he have followed us here?" Tristan asked. "You told me he hated Michel, blamed him for his brother's death. But Michel's back in Tahoe. Why would Davenant be here?" His brows narrowed and he tightened his grip on Mason's jacket sleeve, leaning toward him. "What aren't you telling me?"

"Nothing," Mason replied with a frown and a forceful shrug to break loose of Tristan's grasp. "How the hell should I know what motivates someone like that? The man is a delusional psychopath. His entire clan is. I'd just as soon be able to stop the sunrise with my bare hands as figure out what makes one of the Davenants tick."

"What should we do?" Karen asked, her quiet voice breaking the tension that had grown nearly palpable and strained between the two men. When both Mason and Tristan glanced her way, their severe expressions softened.

"We'll pay for our dinner, then go back to our rooms," Mason said at length, managing a gentle smile as he reached for her, brushing his fingers against her cheek. "I'll call my father and make him aware, see what he wants us to do."

"Great." Tristan rolled his eyes. "That's your answer? Call Michel, let him call the shots, just like always?"

"Yes, unless you've some better alternative in mind," Mason said drily.

"You bet your ass I do. I say you and me, we search this building floor by floor—room by goddamn room, if we have to—and when we find him, we break every bone in his body from about the third cervical vertebra down."

"That won't work," Mason said with a stern glare.

"Why the hell not?" Tristan demanded, and Karen didn't miss the way Mason's eyes darted toward her, then away again, so quick a cut, if she hadn't been standing right there, she might have missed it.

Tristan immediately fell silent, offering no retort, and all at once, she realized.

"Me?" she whispered to Mason, aghast. Shaking her head, she managed a shaky laugh. "That's ridiculous. You think he's after me? Why?"

"Because he's been spying on us long enough to realize that you and Angelina Jones are the only two humans within miles of our compound," Mason said. "And—more importantly—that we care for you. Lina is on her way to Florida right now, but you? You're a seven-hour car trip away. Isn't that what you estimated to reach here, Tristan?"

He doesn't possess the telekinesis of one who has fed from another Brethren, but he's still physically very powerful, Naima had warned her of Jean Luc—and all of a sudden, like a slap in the face, Karen understood the full ramifications of that statement.

He doesn't possess the telekinesis of one who has fed from another Brethren...

"We're getting out of here." Reaching down, Tristan seized Karen by the hand. "Tonight. Right now. We're getting back on the plane and we're flying back to Tahoe."

"My pilot's not available again until Sunday evening," Mason said. "I told him we'd be here for the weekend. He's made plans."

"Then we'll rent a car," Tristan said.

"And take a chance of coming up against one—or more—Davenants on some secluded desert highway in the middle of the night?" Mason frowned. "No, thank you. I'll call Michel, tell him and Naima to drive down tonight. We'll all go back together tomorrow. We're perfectly safe here at the resort in the meantime. The Davenants wouldn't risk trying anything, not with so many possible witnesses about. The threat of exposure's too high. They don't dare."

"Fine," Tristan said. "But I'm not leaving Karen alone tonight."

His fingers tightened firmly against hers, and despite her fear, her mounting anxiety, a sudden, happy little shiver rippled through her.

This machismo bullshit's starting to appeal to me.

It amazed her how nonchalant Mason seemed when their server approached them hesitantly to make sure everything was all right. Nothing but smiles again, he flapped his hand in a dismissive wave as he shooed her and Tristan back upstairs for the night while he settled their bill.

"I'll meet you in Karen's suite. Give me half an hour," he said. "I'll stop off at my room first and give Michel a call."

"Wait a minute—what about the party?" Karen stopped as Tristan again tried to lead her away. "The grand opening celebration. No one there would know me or Tristan, but won't they be expecting you, Mason?"

He chuckled. *"Ma chérie,* you'll give me delusions of grandeur," he said, leaning forward and kissing her cheek. "I'm but one of hundreds of investors, architects, engineers, celebrities, and tight-ass corporate types in designer suits invited to this event. No one will notice my absence, and trust me, even if they did, my associates can more than adequately offer excuses on my behalf."

****

All of the way through the restaurant and lobby to the elevators, Tristan kept Karen pulled close to him in protective proximity, his arm around her or his fingers laced

through her own. She might have enjoyed it more had he
not been so nervous the entire time, his eyes sweeping any
gathering of people with anxious suspicion. They took one
of the glass birdcage elevators up to their floor, and
throughout the ascent, Tristan stood looking outward and
down, his nose nearly pressed to the glass, his gaze cutting a
wide swath across the lobby below.

"He's down there somewhere," he said, so softly, had she
not been standing immediately beside him, she would not
have heard. "I know it."

"Naima said he doesn't have telekinesis," she said.
"Michel doesn't think he's fed from anyone but humans
before. Which sucks for me, I guess—literally—but should
make kicking his ass easier for you."

He shot her a look; her nervous attempt at humor had
obviously fallen flat.

"Thanks," she mumbled, trying a different tack, looking
down at her shoes. "For looking out for me, I mean.
Wanting to keep me safe."

He turned to her fully and when she looked up, hesitant,
she saw he wore a puzzled, somewhat wounded expression.
"That surprises you?"

"No." She shook her head. Even without using
telekinesis, when he wanted to, he could capture her with his
eyes, pinning her, immobilizing her as effectively and

thoroughly as if he'd caught her by the shoulders with his hands. "I mean, I don't know. I guess not."

The elevator chimed softly; they'd reached their floor. The doors slid open, and she took advantage of the distraction to tear her eyes away from his. Without waiting for him, she stepped out into the corridor. For the first time, the long hallways with their intricate, colorful runners and landmarks of nothing but closed doors and brass-plated room numbers seemed somehow ominous. The overhead lights had been dimmed to soft amber hues for the night, but instead of lending a comfortable ambience, the resulting shadows felt foreboding.

"Stay behind me."

She wasn't alone in her caution, she realized, as Tristan brushed past her, catching her by the hand as he flanked her. Macho bullshit or not, she was suddenly grateful to have him feeling protective of her, and stayed close to him as they ventured toward her room together. It wasn't until she slipped her key card into the door and crossed the threshold into the foyer of her suite that she felt able to relax again, to breathe without apprehension.

Tristan didn't share her reassurance. After double-checking the locks on the door as it closed behind them, he walked quickly around the suite, switching on lamps, checking out every alcove and room before satisfying himself that they were alone.

Karen sat in one of the chairs in the living room area and kicked off her shoes. "Now what?" she asked, leaning over and wincing as she rubbed her aching feet each in turn.

"Now we wait," Tristan replied, checking his watch. "Another twenty minutes or so, and Mason should be here."

"You're not happy that he's going to call Michel," she observed.

Shaking his head, he crossed the room and dropped into a chair opposite her. "I still don't see why we need his sanction." With a heavy sigh, he shoved his hair back from his face. "I feel like I can't even take a shit sometimes without Michel's okay."

"It sounds like he's had a lot more experience dealing with the Davenants," she said.

"He's had a lot more experience with a lot of stuff, but that doesn't mean he knows everything. I swear, Karen, I just...I get so tired of everyone kowtowing to him all of the time. Michel thinks because he's the oldest and he controls all of the money, he's some kind of dictator or...or tyrant or something."

His exasperation and frustration were apparent in his face, the pleading look in his eyes. She fought the urge to go to him, to kneel down in front of him and slip her arms around him in a comforting embrace.

"I know," she said quietly.

He cocked his head, then tapped his finger against his throat. "Do you have a safe in here where we could stick that?"

She remembered the Cartier necklace—all forty-six grand worth of it. "Oh, God," she gasped. "Yes, thank you. I'd die if something happened to it."

"You?" he asked with a laugh. "Mason'd be the one footing the bill. And I'm the one he'd make wash dishes to cover it." As she laughed, he rose from his seat. "Here. I'll get it."

Folding his long legs, he squatted in front of her, close enough for her to feel immediately stirred by his sudden, unexpected closeness.

"Turn a little bit," he said, and she pivoted her hips mutely, her posture rigid with sudden bright apprehension. When his hands slipped into her hair, parting it over her shoulders, she melted at the heat of his skin against her neck and shoulders, the friction of his touch. She felt a light tug against her neck as he worked the clasp on the necklace loose, then a faint tickling as he drew it away from her.

"Where's your safe?" he asked, his voice soft, and—was it her imagination?—a bit ragged.

"In the bedroom," she replied, then heard the rustle of his clothing as he stood again. "I set the code already," she called, watching him walk away. "It's one-two-two-six. Twelve twenty-six."

He paused, glancing back at her. "Like December twenty-sixth? That's your birthday."

Inexplicably it pleased her, sending a happy little shiver down her spine to realize he knew the date that she'd been born, had committed it to his memory enough to know it even when mentioned out of proper context.

"You shouldn't use your birthday for PIN numbers or passcodes, you know," he said as he moved again, disappearing into the bedroom and simultaneously dashing that little puddle of giddiness that had only just formed in her belly.

"It's the only way I can keep track of them all," she replied with a frown, because who the hell did he think he was, telling her what she should or shouldn't do?

"It's too easy for someone else to figure out," he called. "You don't..."

His voice faded to momentary silence; then he stepped back into the doorway, looking across the room at her. "Where'd the flowers come from?"

She'd nearly forgotten the box of roses she'd received just before going to dinner.

"Oh." She laughed nervously. "Those? Just from some guy I met on the elevator earlier today."

She started to tell him it was nothing, no big deal, but then he'd uttered a quiet snort of laughter, making her bristle. "Seriously?" he asked. "And now he's sending you roses?"

That this might surprise or even shock him made Karen fume. "Why? Would that bother you?"

His brows shot up in surprise. "Excuse me?"

"I said *would it bother you?*" she snapped. "The idea that another guy might have found me attractive? Just because *you* don't doesn't mean someone else wouldn't."

"Is that what you think?" he asked, and again, like on the elevator, he looked bewildered and hurt.

"What the hell am I supposed to think?" she exclaimed. "You've hardly spoken to me since we left Tahoe, except for tonight at dinner, but you only managed that after you'd knocked back a few glasses of wine. It's always been like that—you either want me around or you push me away. Mason says it's because you're afraid of Michel using me to set you up, but I think it's because you're too damn stubborn to admit when you're wrong, even if that means losing something—or someone—you want."

Someone you love, she added mentally, biting back the words, grateful his telepathy wasn't working so he wouldn't catch that last.

"I don't know what you're talking about," he said, scowling.

"I'm talking about *you* and these stupid games you keep playing. Last week, you almost married another woman, for

Christ's sake! Do you have any idea how that made me feel? Do you even care?"

"Of course I care." He offered this in a quiet voice, one that was edged with remorse and shame. "I didn't marry Tessa."

"Because she couldn't do it," Karen snapped. "Eleanor and Naima told me everything, how they went with Rene to find the two of you, how Tessa left you at the altar."

"That's not what happened." Tristan stiffened, a slight crimp forming between his brows. "*I* was the one who couldn't go through with it, not her."

In that instant, all the wind stripped from Karen's self-righteous sails. Sputtering, she shook her head and blinked stupidly at him. "What?"

"*I* broke off the wedding, not Tessa," he said. "You want to know why? Because when I was filling out the application for our marriage license, I wrote *your name* down, not hers. And she saw me do it. 'Your heart's not in this.' That's what she told me. She said my heart was back in Lake Tahoe." His shoulders sagged as the tension in his body abandoned him, and he stood before her, piteous and vulnerable. "And it was. It still is...with you."

It was a good thing she'd already kicked off the stilettos, she figured, because in that moment, she felt decidedly dizzy. If she'd still been in the high heels, she'd undoubtedly have fallen flat on her ass.

"You're right," he said. "I've been a fool, too scared to admit the truth to myself or to anyone else...but most of all, to you."

"Get out," she whispered, drawing her arms fiercely about herself, because even though he was saying everything she wanted him to say, everything she'd ever hoped he would say, she couldn't accept or believe it. *Not after last night. Not after this morning.*

His brows lifted. "I love you."

"Get out," she said again, more loudly this time.

"I'm not playing games," he insisted. "Karen, please. Last night was amazing. I'd wanted that so much—wanted *you*—for years. Probably from the first time we met."

"Get out!" she shouted, grabbing the nearest potential projectile she could—a decorative vase off a nearby table— and winging it at his head. He ducked to the side, dodging as it blistered past, smashing into the wall behind him and shattering in a spray of bits and pieces. "I don't want to listen to you, not anymore. You broke my heart last week. Then you crushed whatever was left this morning. Don't you get it? Get out of my room. Get out of my life. I'd rather stare down Jean Luc Davenant and a thousand of his brothers than—"

Tristan closed the distance between them in two swift strides, seizing her face between his hands and cutting her voice breathlessly short as he kissed her. His lips pressed fiercely into hers, and she stiffened in wide-eyed surprise.

"I love you," he whispered again, drawing back just enough to speak, keeping his forehead tucked to hers, the tips of their noses brushing. "I've fucked everything up—I know it, and I'm sorry. I know I don't deserve it, but if you give me the chance—I'm begging you, Karen—I'll make it up to you. To my dying breath, every day for the rest of my life, I swear it."

He kissed her again, tilting her face up to him and pulling her near, so she danced on her toes, pressed into his chest. The tip of his tongue grazed the seam of her mouth, and when her lips parted to let him delve inside, she uttered a soft moan, muffled against him. She resisted the indignant urge to push him away and instead let him ease her backward, matching him step for step, until he'd pressed her against the wall. The kiss deepened, his tongue tangling with hers, his hands slipping from her face to her neck, then sweeping down, caressing her shoulders.

He reached behind her for the knot fettering the halter straps of her dress together, pausing to shrug his shoulder and flap his arms to help as she pushed his jacket down, then off. The knot loosened, the straps fell slack, and the twin panels of black silk drooped down from her breasts. His hands fell against her to take the dress's place, massaging slow, sensuous circles, cradling her in his palms.

He dipped his head, his mouth slipping from hers, trailing down her chin, then to her collar. Letting his lips guide the way, he kissed her slowly, until his tongue found her nipple and began to encircle it, slowly at first, then as her heartbeat and breathing grew fluttering and frantic was need, at a quicker, darting pace.

She tilted her head back, leaning into the wall, splaying her fingers through his hair and gasping sharply for breath. While his mouth remained at her breasts, his hands slid down, his fingers closing in the folds of her skirt and lifting it toward her waist. He reached beneath, his hands grazing her upper thighs, then around to her buttocks, easing her into him so that she could feel the strain of his arousal against her through the front of his pants. When he touched the straps of her garters, his fingers lingered, and he groaned, his voice low and filled with need.

Tell me to stop. She waited for him to say this, as he had the night before, because she understood now. He hadn't wanted to bite her, to give in to the bloodlust and feed from her. As he lifted his face to hers again, close enough for his breath the brush through her bangs, she held her breath and waited to hear it.

Tell me to stop.

Then she realized his face, though flushed now, hadn't changed. She could still see the green in his eyes—sharp now, dominating the hazel of his irises in the dim light—

because his pupils hadn't dilated. When he kissed her again, all she felt was the urgent passion in his mouth, not his fangs as they descended. Just as he'd told her at dinner, he was controlling the bloodlust. His body's desire was still evident—and throbbing as it pressed against her apex through the thin covering of her silken panties. But somehow tonight, unlike the night before, he wasn't suffering from the overwhelming, detrimental urge to feed.

Tonight he wants me, she realized, *not my blood.*

Seizing his face between her hands, she kissed him fiercely, deeply, making him whimper against her mouth. When she drew abruptly back, she left him gasping, trembling against her.

"Karen," he whispered, pleading.

"My bedroom," she told him, locking gazes with him, her fingers coiling in his hair again in firm directive. "Now."

CHAPTER ELEVEN

The night before had been rushed, harried; Tristan had been burdened with the bloodlust, fighting against it, and had missed the chance to fully explore and enjoy making love to Karen. It was an oversight he decided to take his time in remedying.

In the bedroom, he shoved the box of roses to the floor with a rustle of tissue paper and a scattering of scarlet petals, then lay her back against the bed, her legs dangling over the side. Hooking his fingers in the fabric of her dress, he pulled it down from her waist. She raised her hips, and it slipped down the lengths of her legs. He cast it aside, then knelt on the floor, pushing her thighs apart, giving him ready access. Leaving her garters in place and the bustier that framed her breasts, he leaned over, easing her panties aside, letting his tongue slip lightly, deliberately between her warm, damp folds.

She gasped at this, stiffening reflexively, then relaxed with a murmur of pleasure as he used his fingers to delve inside her. With his mouth and his hands, he explored her innermost recesses, touching her, tasting her, driving her within moments to a climax that left her writhing on the bed, clutching at his hair.

By this point, his own need had grown so urgent, it was painful. Without bothering to unbutton his shirt, he ripped the front open, then shrugged it loose from his shoulders. She sat up in bed, her hair swept messily about her face, her cheeks flushed and glossy with perspiration. She reached for his belt, the tip of her tongue slipping out of her mouth in a quick, innocent swipe that nearly left him shooting off in his pants like a teenager on prom night.

"God," he groaned, tilting his head back, closing his eyes as she opened his fly and took him into her mouth. Drawing her tongue in sweeping, concentric circles, she teased him, sliding him fully toward the back of her throat, then out again, leaving him breathless. She moved slowly at first, but when he touched her head, guiding her, gently urging her on, she began to move more quickly, bobbing back and forth, drawing him in deeper and deeper each time. When at last he couldn't take any more, he uttered a low cry and caught her shoulders, pushing her away from him and down against the mattress, lowering himself atop her.

Karen's arms encircled his torso, her thighs enveloping his hips, and he let himself sink deeply, fully into her amazing warmth. Sliding in and out of her, slowly so that they could both relish the delicious friction, he kissed her mouth, drawing her tongue against his own. She clutched at his shoulders, then shifted her grip, hooking her fingernails into the meat of his lower back and buttocks, begging him wordlessly to take her harder, faster.

"Don't stop," she pleaded when he obliged, increasing the rhythm at which he plunged into her, listening to the slap of skin against skin, the creaking of the bed beneath them, and her fluttering, quickening mewls.

"Don't stop," she begged, urging him with her hands, driving him into her. He leaned back, grasping her legs, drawing her ankles up to his shoulders, so that each stroke shuddered through her, spearing deep, filling her completely.

She came hard, knotting her hands in the sheets and arching her back as she cried out his name. Her entire body tightened, and she collapsed around him in fierce, rhythmic spasms that made him come without warning. He fell forward, catching himself with his hands spread to frame her face as waves of intense, unbelievable pleasure rocked through him. In its aftermath, he felt spent, exhausted, and crumpled forward, his forehead landing against her shoulder.

He could feel her heart racing, could smell the ambrosia of her sweat on her skin and the blood just beyond, adrenaline-infused and coursing through her. To his surprise—to his absolute amazement—the awareness of this didn't stir the bloodlust at all within him.

Human, he thought, with something akin to wonder as he lifted his head and looked down at her. *This is what it's like to be human.*

She smiled, radiant, breathtaking, and he brushed a strand of wayward hair back from her cheek.

I could get used to this, I think.

He smiled for her, helpless against her, then leaned down to kiss her lightly, sweetly.

"I love you," she whispered, her lips dancing against his own, and in that moment, Tristan had no doubt at all in his heart or mind.

I could definitely get used to this.

****

From the darkness, a muffled digital ring drew Tristan from the depths of sleep.

My phone, he thought dimly as his mind made the groggy, reluctant transition from unconsciousness to alert. Beside him, Karen still slept, her body lying in warm, nearly perfect complement against his own. When he sat up, the sheet drooped away, leaving them both exposed from the waist up, and he blinked stupidly around the dark room, trying to find his cell phone.

I had it in my pocket, he remembered, stumbling out of bed and limping around blindly until he found his pants in a rumpled heap halfway across the room.

He heard Karen murmur softly, incoherently; then the mattress creaked, the covers rustling as she sat up, drawing them modestly to cover her breasts. Squatting, he fished in the pocket of his slacks until he found his phone. When he pulled it out, he saw Mason's number flashing on the caller I.D.

"Shit," he said, because it occurred to him that they'd they'd forgotten completely about Mason's promise to join them once he'd finished talking to Michel on the phone. He glanced over his shoulder at the bedside clock and winced. It was well after midnight; more than three hours had passed since they'd parted company at the restaurant. *And we've been sleeping this whole time. He's probably been and left, beating on the door, wondering where the hell we are.*

"Shit," he said again, thumbing the keypad to answer the call. Raking his fingers through his hair to push it out of his eyes, he tried his best to sound dutifully repentant. "I'm really sorry, Mason," he began.

From the other end of the line, there was nothing but silence. At first. Then, just as he was about to say his uncle's name again, he heard strange sounds, a dull, flat *whap* like a side of beef hitting a concrete floor, followed by the distinctive sound of someone groaning—quiet, choked, pained.

"Mason?" Tristan whispered.

"I'm sorry, poppet," a voice purred in his ear—a voice he recognized from earlier that night. "Mason's a bit...tied up at the moment."

Tristan's brows furrowed, his free hand closing into a sudden, strained fist. All the muscles bridging his shoulders and neck drew instantly taut. "Davenant," he seethed. "You son of a bitch. Where is he? What have you done with him?"

Jean Luc Davenant chuckled gently into the phone. "I haven't done anything *with* him," he said, with feigned insult in his voice. "It's what I've done *to* him that should worry you."

He used to amuse himself by stringing cats upside down from the trees and partially eviscerating them to see how long they could survive, Mason had told Tristan of Jean Luc. *And if they'd resort to eating their own guts to do it.*

"Where is he?" Tristan snapped. For a moment, Jean Luc did nothing but laugh. Furious now, trembling with rage, Tristan screamed into the phone, *"Goddamn you, where's Mason?"*

"Look outside."

Jean Luc's reply came flat, cold from the other end. Tristan blinked in surprise, turning to the nearest floor-to-ceiling window.

"That's right," Jean Luc said. "Walk to the window, poppet. Let me see that pretty face of yours."

Turning again, this time to Karen, Tristan cupped his hand over the phone, pinning her with his stare. *Don't move,* he mouthed. Pointing to the windows to redirect her gaze momentarily, he then mouthed, *He's watching us.*

Her hand darted to her mouth, her face drained of color, the sheet drooping lankly to expose her left breast as she turned it loose.

"Are you there, poppet?" Jean Luc asked.

"Yeah," Tristan growled, stepping into his pants, pulling them up around his hips and buttoning the fly. He went to the window, standing bare chested, vulnerable in front of the tempered glass, staring at his reflection as it floated, ghostlike, against the colorful backdrop of the Las Vegas cityscape below. Facing him was the second Trésor resort tower, an exact mirror image of the building in which he stood. Tristan panned his gaze, struggling to find any hint of Jean Luc's position—a wink of light off the lens of a telescope from a window in the far tower, maybe.

Balling his fist again but leaving his middle finger stiffly extended, he raised his hand, shoving it against the window. "Can you see me, motherfucker?"

Jean Luc laughed. "I want you to listen to me carefully, poppet. You and I are going to play a little game."

"I don't like games."

"That's a shame, because I do. And I'm afraid you're in no position to turn me down."

Another pause; then Tristan heard the muffled whaps again, like someone punching a damp sandbag—only it wasn't a sandbag and he knew it. Mason was the one suffering what sounded like a brutal beating and he remained semilucid, enough in any case, to cry out softly, croaking in feeble protest.

"Stop it!" Tristan slapped his hand against the glass, feeling the thick, heavy panel shudder beneath his palm. "Leave him alone! I'll kill you!"

When Jean Luc returned to the phone, he was chuckling again like a macabre sort of Mrs. Butterworth, filled with grim good humor.

"I'll kill you," Tristan promised. "Do you hear me, you sick bastard?"

"Are you ready to play?" Jean Luc asked, unfazed.

"Go fuck yourself."

This time, there were no sounds of landing blows, but from the other end of the line, Mason began to shriek, his voice ripping up shrill, agonized octaves loud enough for Karen to hear, even from the bed. Tristan could see her reflected horror through the glass, heard the sharp, aghast intake of her breath.

"Stop," Tristan cried. "Stop it, stop it, you son of a bitch! *Mason!*"

The screams cut abruptly short, and somehow that silence was even more terrifying to Tristan. He heard a soft rustle, then an audible click as Jean Luc picked up the phone.

"Did you catch all of that, poppet? I can do some more if you need me to."

"You touch him again, and I'll rip your arms out of your goddamn sockets, cram them hand-first up your—"

"Are you ready to play?" Jean Luc interjected mildly.

Tristan blinked at Karen, then turned around again. "Yes," he whispered, nodding once. "Whatever you want. Just leave Mason alone. All right?" His voice grew strained, and he closed his eyes. "Please. Don't hurt him anymore."

"Splendid," Jean Luc purred, the tone of his voice lending itself to a malicious sort of smile. "Listen closely, then, because I'll only do this once. You get it right—you be a good little poppet and do exactly as you're told—and your dear uncle walks out of here with little more than a limp to show for his trouble. Get it wrong—if you even think about fucking with me—then I will remove each of his vital organs forcibly and in turn, using only the crudest of surgical methods and foregoing any benefit of anesthesia. Do you understand?"

Through the glass, Tristan looked at Karen, frozen with fear on the bed. She may not have been privy to the entire conversation, but she'd gleaned enough—primarily from his own reactions—to get the gist of it.

"Yes," he said, because the son of a bitch hadn't mentioned her, and Tristan meant to keep it that way; keep Davenant distracted from her for however long it took to make sure she remained safe, out of harm's way. "Tell me what to do."

****

"Lock the door behind me," Tristan told Karen as he stood at the threshold less than ten minutes later, ready to leave. "The deadbolt too. Don't open it for anyone or any reason. Not until Michel and Naima get here. Do you understand?"

He'd given her instructions to call his grandfather, fill him in on their situation.

"What difference will it make?" she asked, because she'd been trying her damndest to convince him not to go. "It's like you and Mason both said earlier. They're seven hours away. They'd have to drive all night and—"

"We don't have a choice." Tristan cut her short by pressing his fingertips against her lips. "He's got Mason," he said, his eyes round, frightened and pleading. "I can't sit here and wait for the cavalry while that son of a bitch is up there doing Christ only knows what to him."

By *up there*, he meant the rooftop of the opposing Trésor tower. He'd told her that was where Jean Luc Davenant had instructed him to go. There was nothing up there but heating and air-conditioning units, electrical conduits, assorted pipes, and ventilation shafts. It would be isolated and empty, and she was terrified for him.

"Tristan." Catching him by the arm, she tried to pull him back into the room. "You said you don't have any powers, remember?"

Because if he'd been able to use his extrasensory abilities, she might not have been so worried. With telekinesis, he had considerably more strength than on his own, even with his naturally enhanced Brethren physiology. She'd seen him move his truck with his mind using the same deliberate ease that he'd use to play *Für Elise* by rote.

"Hey." He tried to smile for her, cupping his hand to her face. "You said he doesn't either. Remember?" Leaning down, he kissed her softly, sweetly against the mouth. "Call Michel. Tell him to get here as fast as he can, however he can. I'll do my best to leave him some ass-beating leftovers."

She began to cry, seizing him around the neck in a sudden, fierce embrace, shuddering against his shoulder. "Be careful."

"I will," he said, muffled, into her hair. As he drew back, he kissed her again, deeper this time, fervent and desperate.

"I love you," she whispered.

"I love you too."

She held on to his hand for as long as she could, until only their fingertips lingered, hooked together, then slipped apart. Her arm remained outstretched, her hand reaching for him, her vision blurred with tears as he walked away.

When he was gone, she shut the door, throwing the deadbolt home, as he'd instructed. Except for the bedroom, all the draperies in the suite had been closed, but she still felt as though she was being watched, that somehow even now, Jean Luc was monitoring their every move, hers and Tristan's, however separate.

Sitting on the floor, crouched beside the cover of one of the couches, she used her cell phone's memory function to call Michel. It was late and Michel was obviously asleep; the line rang and rang, and she began to panic, thinking he wouldn't answer, that it would roll over to voice mail and he wouldn't realize that she'd called until the following morning.

Oh, please, she thought, closing her eyes as new tears streamed down her cheeks and she pressed her lips tightly together to muffle a miserable sob. *Please, please, oh, God, Michel, please pick up.*

As if he'd read her mind all the way from the shores of Lake Tahoe, Michel answered the phone. After a loud series of rustles and thuds, his voice croaked over the line, hoarse and sleepy. "Hullo?"

"Michel?" Karen began to weep, loudly, strained, and clapped her hand over her mouth.

"Karen?" Recognizing her voice—and obviously alarmed by her tears—he spoke sharply. "Is that you? What is it? What's wrong?"

"You have to help us," she begged. "Please, Michel, you have to come. You have to leave right now!"

****

It would have been so much easier if Tristan had been able to use his telepathy. He could have used it to manipulate one of the hotel employees into giving him a passkey to the service entries and exits, just as he'd convinced the pharmacy technician in Lake Tahoe that the name on his driver's license had been *Brandon Noble,* not his own.

But because he couldn't do this, he had to improvise once he'd reached the top floor in the second Trésor tower, then force his way from there through a steel door conspicuously marked EMERGENCY USE ONLY.

He may not have been able to wield his telepathy, but as a Brethren, he was still stronger than the average bear. Glancing quickly around to make sure he was unobserved, he rammed his shoulder forcefully into the door. It took three such attempts before at last, the lock gave way and snapped. The door swung open and he stumbled across the threshold into another shadow-draped stairwell, this one with a simple flight of metal grid stairs leading up to an exterior door.

Getting close, Tristan thought, because he had that peculiar prickling sensation racing along his nerve endings again, that extrasensory awareness of another like himself in his immediate proximity. Stepping into the alcove, he caught the door behind him with his hand, letting it close softly and latch back into proper place.

The posh décor of the resort didn't extend to this area. The walls were cinderblock, painted an industrial shade of gray. Mounted on one opposite the staircase was a bright red, square metal case. *FIRE BOX* had been painted across the front panel in yellow stenciled letters.

Tristan went to the box and tried to open it but found it locked. With a wary look up at the exit door, he hooked his fingers beneath the sharp edge of the panel, gritted his teeth, and gave a mighty yank. The little locking mechanism popped as readily as the door's had, and the front of the box swung open wide.

"Hot damn," Tristan whispered, because he'd hoped to find something he could use as a weapon inside. To that point, he'd seen nothing more promising than a house phone or fake

ficus trees in the hotel hallways along his way. But mounted inside of the red fire box was an ax, its long handle painted yellow, its double-sided head—one with a cutting blade, the other with a spike—painted to match the box that housed it.

I bet I can do some damage with this.

With another jerk, Tristan snapped the straps of metal securing it into place and hefted it in hand. It wasn't much, but it was sharp, potentially lethal, and better than going up against Jean Luc Davenant with his bare hands and a bad attitude.

Carrying the ax, he turned, then started up the metal stairs.

"Come alone. Come quickly," Jean Luc had told him on the phone. "I'll be waiting on the roof, but not for very much longer. You have twenty minutes to get here. Run, poppet, run."

He glanced at his watch. Less than five minutes left. He'd dressed hurriedly back in Karen's suite, barking directions to her the entire time. She'd been frightened and upset, and he'd struggled against the urge to waste even more precious time than he already had by trying to comfort her. He'd wound up sprinting across the courtyard separating the twin resort buildings. The grand-opening celebration had been in full swing by that point, and he'd shoved his way through a raucous crowd of partygoers and guests to reach the elevators. It felt like it had stopped at every floor in its descent, and exasperated, running out of time, Tristan had finally fought his way off, then raced up the stairs for the remaining floors.

He could feel his shirt sticking to his skin between his shoulder blades and beneath his arms with sweat. When he shoved his hair back from his face, his fingers shaking anxiously, he found it damp too.

I'm coming, Mason, he thought as he reached the top of the stairs. Raising the ax above his shoulder, poised at the ready, he prepared himself to batter down the steel door. To his surprise, when he pushed against the latch, he found it unlocked, and it swung wide obligingly, letting in a sudden cool burst of nighttime air.

Cautiously, cutting his gaze in a broad arc, he stepped out onto the roof. Gravel crunched underfoot. Moths danced and flitted in the broad swath of illumination cast by a bright, glaring security bulb mounted directly above his head. Tristan's shadow first pooled beneath him, then stretched out long, taffylike, as he broke away from the threshold. Spotlights had been strategically positioned around the ground level of both towers to showcase the grand-opening spectacle, and their pale beams speared up and into the sky, reaching seemingly into infinity overhead.

He grasped the handle of the ax lightly in both hands and crept forward, panning his gaze, squinting to peer into the heavy shadows all around him.

I'll be waiting on the roof, Jean Luc had told him, offering no other specifics besides this. When he saw no hint of movement, no other signs of life except that nagging, electrified sensation simmering beneath his skin, he frowned.

"I'm here," he called out. Pivoting in a slow circle, he made certain to double-check behind him. "Hey, Davenant. I'm here. Come on out."

I've got a little surprise for you, he thought with a humorless smile, shifting his grip on the ax handle.

From his left, behind a tangle of pipes and vent shafts, he heard a low groan. *Mason,* he realized, turning smoothly on his heel and racing in the direction of the sound.

"Mason," he shouted. "Mason, I'm coming. I'm..."

His voice faltered as he ducked beneath some conduits and caught sight of his uncle below. "Oh, Jesus," he whispered, stricken, the ax nearly tumbling from his fingers in his horrified shock.

He scrambled around the remaining pipes to reach the straight-backed wooden chair to which Mason had been bound. He'd been hog-tied, his wrists lashed together behind him, connected with a taut strap of rope to similar bindings around his ankles. His shirt had been torn open, the dark panels splayed wide to reveal the pale skin of his chest, which stood out in ghoulish and apparent contrast to the massive amounts of blood that were smeared down his torso and abdomen.

"Mason!" Dropping the ax, Tristan fell to his knees in front of his uncle. Mason's head had drooped down, his chin nearly to his chest, and Tristan lifted his face, cradling it between his hands. He'd been savagely beaten, his face battered and scraped into a bloodied, bruised, and nearly unrecognizable mess. At first, Tristan couldn't even tell if Mason was breathing or not, until he leaned forward, frantic, terrified, and felt blood bubble out from between his uncle's lips to pepper his cheek.

"Mason, can you hear me?" Using one hand to hold Mason's head up, Tristan used the pad of his thumb to gently peel back his eyelid. Mason groaned again, faint and feeble, but otherwise remained unresponsive. There was still no sign of Jean Luc, and Tristan rose to his feet long enough to backpedal and retrieve the ax.

"Hang on," he said, even though Mason's chin had fallen once more and he sat, lank, limp and still in his bonds. "I'm going to get you out of here, Mason. Just hang on."

He squatted behind the chair, holding the ax near the top of the shaft so he could saw at the ropes with the razor-sharp edge of the blade. He caught a glimpse of something small and white lying in a puddle of blood on the ground. Frowning, he reached for it.

Oh, Jesus, he thought, his eyes widening as he lifted in hand what looked like a tooth that had been forcibly pulled from its socket—a canine tooth, too unnaturally elongated to have come from anyone human.

"Jesus Christ." He gasped aloud when he saw a second tooth, torn free and discarded, on the ground beneath

Mason's chair. Beside it, hidden beneath the shadows of the chair seat from immediate view, was a pair of pliers.

On his hands and knees, he scuttled back to face his uncle, again cupping Mason's face between his hands.

"Mason," he whispered, stricken and dismayed. Gently, gingerly, he touched Mason's mouth, easing his upper lip back. When he saw the ruins of Mason's mouth, the bloody, raw, ragged holes at the outermost edge of his upper palate, he uttered a soft, anguished cry. "Oh, God, what did he do to you?"

Mason's eyelids fluttered, then opened to a bleary half-mast. "Tristan..." His voice was ragged, little more than a croak.

"I'm here." Tristan leaned forward, kissing his brow, smoothing his blood-matted hair back from his face. "I'm here, Mason," he said again, on the verge of tears. "It's all right now. Hang on. I'm going to get you out of..."

He fell silent, bewildered, as his hand slipped to the side of Mason's neck and he felt something there, torn flesh and damp warmth beneath. As he drew his fingers away, he saw a pair of dime-sized wounds, parallel to each other, that had been punched into the meat of his uncle's neck.

"Tristan," Mason whispered again just as Tristan realized, to his horror:

Holy shit, Davenant fed from him!

"Get...out of here..." Mason pleaded. But even as the words were out of his mouth, Tristan felt the air around him abruptly collapse, like a gigantic invisible hand clamping fiercely around him, hoisting him into the air.

He didn't even have time to cry out. In an instant, he was airborne, hurtling backward at an unbelievable rate of speed, slamming hard into a cinderblock wall. He struck hard enough to snap ribs; he felt them go at about the same time as he heard the telltale *crunch,* and a bright swell of molten agony ripped through his torso, stripping the breath from him. The back of his head smashed into the concrete with enough force to leave him seeing stars. When the telekinetic grip on him relinquished, he collapsed in a heap in the pool of pale security light, facedown and groaning.

For a long moment, there was nothing but the pain and the dizzying sensation as his poor mind tried not to swim away into shadows. Clapping his hand to his brow, he tried to sit up but bit back a cry as pain lanced through his injured chest for the effort.

Then he heard the soft crunch of shoe soles against the cold, hard surface of the roof. His vision bleary, his mind reeling, he looked up to see a man walking toward him. At first more silhouette than discernable form, he was tall and lean, his gait comfortable and leisurely. When he stepped into the circumference of light and it spilled over his face,

Tristan saw dark hair swept back from his face and dark eyes framed with murderous intensity by low-slung brows.

The man approached, then squatted down next to Tristan. Reaching down, he closed his fist in Tristan's hair, wrenching his head back, nearly ripping his scalp raw. Tristan gritted his teeth against another anguished cry as the sudden movement sent another shudder of pain through his shattered ribs.

"My God, you look just like your father," Jean Luc Davenant remarked, the ferocity in his gaze contrasted by the gentle uplift to the corner of his mouth. With a chuckle, he leaned over. "Oh, I am going to enjoy this," he promised, his lips and breath brushing with obscene intimacy as he whispered into Tristan's ear. "Each and every excruciating moment."

CHAPTER TWELVE

If only I'd brought my gun, Karen thought as she shouldered her way through the crowd of party guests in the tower lobby. Not that she made a habit of traveling with the .257 within ready reach, like she was Annie Oakley or something, but because she felt naked and vulnerable without something even remotely resembling a weapon in her hands.

"Slow down, *ma chérie,*" Michel had said to her over the phone. "I can't understand you. What's happened? Tell me what's wrong."

She'd still been tearful but choked down her sobs, dragged her hands across her cheeks to dry them, and forced herself to get her shit together. "Jean Luc Davenant's here," she'd said. "He's here in Las Vegas. He must have followed us somehow. I don't know. But he's taken Mason."

"Where's Tristan?" Michel had said, his voice edged with an uncharacteristic frenetic anxiety that bordered on outright panic.

"He's gone to help Mason," she'd replied.

"What?" Michel's voice had scraped up shrill octaves.

"Davenant told him to meet them on top of the second resort tower."

"Mon Dieu," Michel had breathed from the other end of the line, clearly stricken. *My God.*

"His powers aren't working, Michel," she'd told him. "He told us earlier, he's taken some medication Brandon Noble told him about to control his bloodlust, and it's dampened his telepathy somehow, his telekinesis. He's going in there blind."

"Mon Dieu," Michel had whispered again. "How long ago did he leave?"

"Not long. Maybe five, ten minutes."

There was a momentary silence, and she'd been acquainted with him long enough to guess as to what he was doing out of habit—pacing, combing his fingers through his hair, tugging anxiously at his beard. At length, he'd spoken again, but this time, his voice was small, pleading. "You can still catch him, then."

"What?" Karen had blinked stupidly.

"I'm leaving now," Michel had told her, and sure enough, she'd heard the jingle of car keys, the rustle of fabric as he'd hurriedly dressed. "I'll get there as soon as I can, but Tristan needs help now. Run after him, Karen. Stop him if you can."

How am I supposed to do that? she'd wanted to ask, because nobody knew better than Michel that Tristan was difficult, impossible even, to dissuade once he'd set his mind on something.

"Tell him I'm coming," Michel had said. "I'm on my way. But hurry, Karen. You have to go now. You have to catch him."

"What about Davenant?" Karen had already been on her feet and in motion, rushing back to the bedroom and throwing open her bag, grabbing the sweater and jeans she'd worn on the plane. Wriggling, hopping from one foot to the other, and strategically ducking her head, she'd managed to re-dress while keeping the phone tucked to her ear as she spoke. "Mason said he's after me, that you and Naima found him last night in the woods by my house."

"*Quoi?*" Michel had asked. *What?*

She'd paused, balancing heronlike on one leg as she'd crammed her shoes back on. "That's why we came here," she'd said slowly, puzzled by his reaction, the bewilderment she'd heard in his voice. "To Las Vegas. Mason said you'd told him to take me away from the compound to keep me safe."

From the other end of the phone, she'd heard a soft, almost rueful chuckle. Then Michel had said, "*Ma chérie,* I've no doubt that Mason wanted to keep you in safe company."

There had been a peculiar edge to his words, and she'd frowned. "But..." she'd said, letting the word draw out for a prolonged moment. "That's not why Mason brought me along, is it?"

With sudden horror, she'd realized. *It's not me. It hasn't been me all along. Jean Luc Davenant wasn't in the woods watching my house—watching me.*

She shoved her way into the first crowded but available elevator car she could find, and watched in growing dismay as other passengers pushed buttons, lighting up nearly every floor between the lobby and the roof.

It's going to take me forever to get up there, she thought, pressing her lips together to stifle a groan. It was hot and cramped once the doors slid closed, with everyone knocking shoulders, jockeying for space. The intermingling smells of perfume, cologne, champagne, and sweat hung stagnant in the air.

But hopefully it's taking Tristan that long too, she thought, watching anxiously as the numbers lit up in a row above the doors, marking the progress of their ascent. *God, I hope so. Please let me reach him in time.*

****

Tristan cried out, breathless and choked, as he slammed into the ground, landing heavily in front of Mason's chair. He'd lost count of how many times Jean Luc had thrown him telekinetically, or how many walls he'd smashed into.

He heard the scuff of Jean Luc's footsteps drawing near, and uttered a soft, miserable groan as the other man snatched a fistful of his hair again and jerked, craning his head back, forcing the ends of his shattered ribs to grind together. To that point, he hadn't fought back, hadn't been able to, but furious determination welled up in him. With a ragged cry, he rammed his elbow back, catching Jean Luc squarely in the gut, forcing him to stagger breathlessly backward.

Even though it hurt, Tristan forced himself to move, to roll over, scramble to his feet. He didn't give Davenant the chance to recover his wind or wits, and swung his fist around, plowing his knuckles into the bridge of his nose. Jean Luc's head snapped back on his neck and he stumbled, crashing down onto his ass.

"You...son of a bitch," Tristan said, reaching down, grabbing the fire ax from near Mason's chair where he'd left it. Hoisting it above his head, clasping the handle between both hands, he readied himself to swing it down, to bury the broad blade into the dead center of Jean Luc's forehead. "You son of a—"

Jean Luc may not have had his telekinetic powers long, but he wielded them with brutal abandon. As if struck headlong by an invisible Mack truck, Tristan flew backward, plowed away from Jean Luc, the ax knocked from his hands. More ribs splintered as again he struck the wall, but before he could even hit the ground, he was jerked forward, an unwilling marionette pulled in relentless, unwavering tow back to Mason's chair, back to where he'd started.

"You've got fire in you, poppet," Jean Luc remarked with a laugh, smirking even as he touched the now crooked, swollen tip of his nose, his fingertips coming away smeared with blood. "I'll give you that."

Tristan grunted, breathless, as invisible hands hoisted him aloft, dangling him at least a foot off the ground, then forced his arms out in a cruciform posture. Slowly, he rotated in a semicircle, coming around to face his uncle.

"Such a pity to have to extinguish it," Davenant said. Then Tristan screamed as his left arm abruptly twisted into an unnatural shape, new joints seeming to form as bones simultaneously snapped beneath his skin like dry-rotted wood at Jean Luc's mental command.

"Tristan!" Mason cried out, twisting against his bonds. He was too weak from blood loss to summon any of his own telepathic or telekinetic abilities; his physical strength had been stripped to nearly that of a newborn kitten.

Once released from Jean Luc's telekinetic hold, Tristan crashed to the ground, landing on his belly, shuddering with pain as he tried vainly to move his shattered arm.

"What do you say, Mason?" Jean Luc's voice was still filled with irrepressible, sadistic good cheer, and with a loud stomp, he planted one foot on either side of Tristan, so he squatted, straddling the younger man. "Shall I bleed him here in front of you? He's young yet, his blood still sweet, I'm willing to bet." The corners of his mouth turned down in a grimace, and he spat. "Not like yours."

"Please." Mason gasped. "Whatever you want...I'm right here. Do it to me. The boy is no part of this."

"He's *every goddamn part of this*," Jean Luc seethed. "A brother for a brother, Mason. A son for a son. That's the oath I swore to my father and the rest of my kin. I thought we'd settled that debt in 1815 when we torched your family's home to the ground—with the miserable lot of you presumably inside. Imagine our surprise to recently learn, then, of your survival."

He wrenched against Tristan's hair again, making him cry out. "Did you know, poppet, that in the year 1793, when I was little more pup than you are now, my brother Victor stood in a duel where Michel Morin was his opponent's second? Though he drew first blood, Victor took a shot in the chest and Michel, foregoing his own oath as a Brethren healer, left him in the field to die in disgrace. And then this son of a bitch"—again yanking Tristan's hair, Jean Luc forced him to look at Mason—"was called to tend to Victor in his father's stead. Only he failed."

"I'm sorry." Mason gasped. "I...I've told you...the damage was too great. There was nothing I could do. I tried..."

"Victor was a good man, a loyal son, a loving brother!" Jean Luc shouted, cutting him short. "You let him linger there for twenty-three minutes, writhing in pain, before his lungs filled with blood and he drowned!"

He opened his hand, and Tristan crumpled to the pavement. Lifting his head, weak and dazed, he watched Jean Luc approach Mason's chair.

He's crazy, he thought dimly. *Just like Naima said: feral psychosis. He's drained Mason nearly dry and hasn't fed from one of us before. It's affecting his mind, making him delusional.*

"And for each of those twenty-three minutes, I plan to enjoy ten years' worth of vengeance against the both of you." Jean Luc began to pace, slow, slinking circles treacherously close to Mason's seat, directing his comments in a low purr. "I'm going to take my time with your pretty little poppet, break him measure by measure, until there's nothing left but form and flesh—his mind so scarred and scraped hollow from two hundred and thirty years of relentless, unimaginable torment, he'll never recover. And then when I'm finished—when I've fed from him, fucked him, and had my fill of him in any other possibly conceivable fashion—I'll send him home to you and Michel with a bow around his neck and a tube to feed him through. Because the two of you let Victor die. A brother for a brother. A son for a son. That's what I mean to collect tonight."

Tristan laughed, ignoring the pain that shot through his torso for the effort. Jean Luc froze in midstep and both he and Mason blinked at him in mutual, stupefied surprise.

"You need...to get off the farm more often, hayseed," he rasped. "My father...has been dead for more than thirty years."

When Jean Luc continued looking at him, his expression caught somewhere between incredulous and furious, he couldn't help himself and laughed again. "Surprise, dipshit. Arnaud Morin shot himself in the head...at some piss-rot motel in the French Quarter...in 1975."

"Arnaud?" After another bewildered moment, realization seemed to dawn on Jean Luc, and he tipped back his head, laughing. "You mean your half-wit, drunkard brother?" he asked Mason, slapping him on the back of the head as if sharing some hilarious joke with him. "Is that what you've told him all of these years?"

"Shut your mouth," Mason said.

Confused, Tristan looked at his uncle. *What is he talking about?* he thought, but Mason wouldn't look at him, had, in fact, turned his face defiantly away from Jean Luc, his brows furrowed, his eyes and lips clamped tightly shut.

Still laughing, Jean Luc came to stand in front of Tristan, then folded his legs beneath him, lowering himself to look almost tenderly down at him. "Poor poppet," he said. "You really don't know, do you?"

175

"You...son of a bitch," Mason cried. "Leave him alone! You've...no right—"

"Haven't you ever looked in the mirror?" Jean Luc asked Tristan with a gentle smile. "I could tell from the first time I laid eyes on you. Arnaud Morin didn't sire you. His father did."

Tristan flinched as if he'd been struck again. *What?* he thought, stunned. *But that...that would mean...*

Jean Luc seized him in a sudden telekinetic hold, jerking him to his feet and shoving him face-first toward Mason, holding him pinned in the air, immobilized, nearly nose to nose with his uncle.

"Tell him, Mason," Jean Luc said. "Tell him it's the truth."

"Mason?" Tristan said, stricken. *Tell me it's not,* he pleaded in his mind. *Tell me it's a lie, Mason. Oh, God, please tell me you haven't lied to me my whole life—not you, anyone but you. Tell me Michel's not my father.*

"Michel loved your mother," Mason said. "Tristan, listen to me...he and Lisette loved each other deeply, but they always knew...because of Phillip...they knew they couldn't..."

"No," Tristan whispered, shaking his head. "No, no, that's not true. That can't be true."

"I'm sorry." Mason's eyes flooded with tears. "God above, *mon lapin*, I...I'm so sorry. We were only trying to protect you."

"And a damn fine job you've done of it too," Jean Luc lauded from behind them.

Tristan uttered a startled yelp as he abruptly flew backward, crashing hard into the wall, this time cracking more ribs and catching the brunt of the blow on his already battered arm. With a hoarse, agonized cry, he collapsed, on the brink of unconsciousness, his mind succumbing to shadows. He didn't hear Jean Luc's approach but was shocked back to semi-lucidity by pain as the older man snatched him by the hair again, hoisting his head from the ground.

"No, no, no," he said, clucking his tongue, mock-fussing. "Don't fade out on me now, poppet. I want you wide awake for this."

Tristan groaned, breathless and hurting, as Jean Luc forced him onto his knees. Spreading his feet wide as he stood behind Tristan, Jean Luc pulled his head back, angling his face toward the sky. With his free hand, he gestured in Mason's direction, and the pliers Tristan had seen beneath the chair rose into the air, wobbling unsteadily in place before floating toward Mason's outstretched, awaiting palm.

"I'm going to rip out his teeth," Jean Luc said to Mason.

Dazed with pain, Tristan looked up and saw the glow of stars overhead and the broad, bright sweep of each spotlight beam cutting intersecting diagonals within his line of sight. He felt Jean Luc's hand slip from his hair, then come around beneath his chin to crush against his jaw, forcing his mouth open.

"Not just his fangs," Jean Luc said. "Every last goddamn one of them." With a grim wink delivered for Tristan's exclusive benefit, he added, "That way, whenever I skull-fuck him, he won't be able to bite."

As he felt Jean Luc cram the pliers past his lips, Tristan tried to focus his waning conscious awareness on the stars, how their pinpoints of light reminded him of the glistening beads of dewy glow on Karen's skin when she'd become aroused, when his pupils had widened and the bloodlust had come upon him, expanding his sensitivity to light. He thought of Karen because he imagined he could feel her, that inherent sensation he'd always felt. He imagined he could smell her sweet, delicate fragrance, the one he'd know anywhere, the one he hoped to cement in his mind, to cling to for comfort throughout whatever unimaginable hell he was about to endure.

I'm sorry, he thought, closing his eyes tightly. *Oh, God, Karen, I'm sorry I never fed from you, never had the courage to see our pair-bonding through. If I had, I'd be able to sense you now—for real, not just my imagination—and I could tell you that I love you.*

I love you too, he thought he heard her say, her voice inside his mind, and then his eyes flew wide as he heard her with his ears too, a furious cry from somewhere behind him. Jean Luc jerked abruptly, violently, his hands falling away from Tristan, the pliers clattering to the ground. Tristan fell forward, catching himself with his uninjured arm before he face-planted into the asphalt again. Cradling his broken arm against his belly, he looked over his shoulder in bewildered surprise.

He saw Karen standing there, bathed in a corona of light from the security lamp. There was blood on her face, a light spattering of dark splotches, as if it had somehow splashed onto her. Her brows were furrowed with a murderous ferocity he would never have expected or thought her capable of.

As she stumbled back, Jean Luc in turn floundered forward, his eyes wide, his mouth agape, a strange caw escaping from his lips. He pivoted clumsily, trying to face her, and Tristan saw something long and thick, a shaft of bright yellow dangling parallel to the length of his spine.

"You..." Jean Luc croaked at Karen. "You...human bitch!"

With that, he pitched forward, crashing to the ground, the spiked end of the fire ax buried deeply in the back of his skull. She'd swung it hard enough to split the bone open wide, like a rotten walnut, and he lay prone and motionless on the ground, blood pooling out to envelop him in a widening circumference.

"Karen?" Tristan gasped in shock, certain that he was either dreaming—that he'd passed out somewhere along the line—or was suffering from pain-induced hallucinations.

"I'm here." She rushed toward him, dancing around Jean Luc's outstretched legs, then falling onto her knees. Her arms flew around him and he crumpled into her shoulder, shuddering in her embrace. "Oh, God," she whispered, even as his consciousness at last abandoned him fully, and he fainted in her arms. "I'm here, Tristan. It's all right. It's over now."

CHAPTER THIRTEEN

"He didn't sense me," Karen said to Michel as the two of them sat together on opposite sides of Tristan's bed more than a week later. She couldn't come up with any other reason why she'd been able to take Jean Luc Davenant wholly by surprise. "I'm not one of the Brethren, so he wasn't even aware of me. He couldn't sense my presence."

"He was too busy focusing on revenge," Michel said, his expression fraught with guilt and remorse as he watched Tristan sleep.

"He's my son," Michel had told Karen at the Trésor, an admission so frank and unexpected, she'd nearly keeled over in shock. "He doesn't know. Mason does, but no one else, not in the entire clan. If Jean Luc Davenant figures it out..." His voice had grown strained, and he'd paused for a long moment as if composing himself again. "Please," he'd whispered to Karen. "Help my sons."

He hadn't had time that horrific night to explain to her more fully than this, but during the long days that had followed, during which Tristan had languished, comatose

and unresponsive, in the compound medical clinic back in
Lake Tahoe, the two of them had had ample opportunity to
talk.

Tristan had been injured so badly, had he been human,
in all likelihood he wouldn't have survived. A chest tube had
been inserted to ease the burden on his right lung, which
had been punctured by his broken ribs and subsequently
collapsed. Severe brain contusions had resulted in prolonged
unconsciousness and intracranial swelling. He'd also
suffered moderate renal injury and a dislocated hip and
shoulder. Michel had personally performed the numerous
surgical procedures needed to repair these injuries, plus try
to restore eventual functioning and strength to Tristan's
shattered arm.

He'd kept a faithful vigil at the younger man's bedside,
leaving only to check on Mason. Although badly beaten,
Mason had a far better prognosis than Tristan. He'd spent
only two nights at the clinic before Michel had discharged
him, and he'd been in earlier that morning to show off a set
of prosthetic teeth that had been fitted to replace the fangs
Jean Luc had so viciously excised.

"I've got my everyday pair," he'd said, flashing Karen a
grin that might have been handsome, had it not been for the
healing bruises and abrasions still apparent on his face. "And
these"—holding out his hand, he'd shown her a removable

bridge fitted with a pair of long, gold-plated canines—"for more formal occasions."

"You saved Mason's life," Michel murmured, looking across Tristan's bed at her. His voice was soft and somewhat strained, as if he hovered on the verge of tears. "And Tristan's too. I can't thank you enough."

Karen shook her head. "There's no need."

"Yes," Michel replied. "There is. I've seen the way Tristan looks at you. I've sensed his thoughts, the conflict he feels inside." A soft smile played at the corners of his mouth. "Just as I've sensed your own."

"I love him," Karen said. It felt good to admit this aloud—and to Michel of all people—right somehow in her heart.

"I know," he said. "You may find this hard to believe, but I've been in love before, enough to recognize it when I see it. A long time ago, before we left Kentucky, my father had a slave girl named Rachel who worked in the kitchen. She was exquisite, quite possibly the most amazing creature God ever saw fit to grace upon this earth. Of course, things being how they were in those days, I'd have been no more free to love her openly as a human than as a Brethren. So I loved her in secret, and for her part, she loved me in return." His gaze became distant and he fell momentarily silent, glancing down at the bed, and Tristan's fingers, laced loosely through his own.

"Was that what made you think of the pair-bonding concept?" she asked, making him smile.

"Who told you about that?"

"Mason," she said, and he chuckled.

"I might have guessed. Yes, she's the reason. Or the inspiration, I guess you could say."

"Did you feed from her?"

"Like a glutton. Whenever I could." He laughed again. "She never minded for it, said it aroused in her a sort of wildness for me, made her damn near insatiable." Cutting her a sheepish look, he said, "Though I suppose you don't really want to hear about that."

Karen shook her head. "I don't mind. What happened to her?"

His smile withered. "She died. I guess as all of us must at some point. But when she did, it left behind an emptiness inside of me. Something dark and hollow, hurting. I didn't think I would ever love again...not like with Rachel."

Again, his attention turned to Tristan, and he drew his thumb lightly against the unconscious younger man's knuckles. "But I was wrong. When my oldest son, Phillip— you've met him, haven't you? Once or twice?—when he was wed to Lisette Giscard, when I set eyes on this delicate, gentle flower of a woman for the first time, it felt like a punch to my heart, as if all of the emotions, the attraction, the desire I'd once felt for Rachel were instantaneously resurrected. She was extraordinary."

Again he smiled. "She would play for me for hours on the piano. *Mon Dieu,* I could never tire of listening to her play. She's the one who taught Tristan, you know, although she'd have told you he was the more talented between them. Phillip always found it trifling, and he seldom paid mind to it...or her. She suffered a miscarriage, their first child, and he all but shunned her after that. She was his first wife, but he'd relegated her in his regard to less than any of the others, incompetent somehow. An inconvenience to him. She turned to me for comfort and affection, and I'm ashamed to admit it, *ma chérie,* but I gave it to her willingly, gladly."

"What about Arnaud?" Karen asked.

His expression shifted, growing ashamed. "He hardly knew her. By that point, his alcohol abuse was out of control. I could count on one hand the number of days I found him sober in that year alone. It was Lisette's idea to say they'd had an affair when she became pregnant. She remembered the fire of 1815, and all of the infighting that precipitated it. She was terrified that if I admitted to being the father of her unborn child, it would all start again, creating a schism in the clan from which we'd never recover." Shaking his head, he heaved a sigh. "I don't know. Maybe she was right. But agreeing to that—denying her and

Tristan—was the hardest decision I've ever made in my life...and one I still question and regret to this day."

From the bed, Tristan uttered a soft sound, breathless and hurting, his brows lifting in his sleep as he moved his head restlessly. Karen and Michel sprang to their feet in unison, both of them leaning over the side rails.

"Easy, *petit,*" Michel murmured, smoothing Tristan's hair back from his brow. "It's all right. You're safe now." When he looked up at Karen, she saw tears swimming in his eyes, gleaming with reflected light. "I love him too," he whispered.

She smiled and reached for him, giving his hand a gentle squeeze. "I know."

****

"He needs to feed."

Michel had told her this before excusing himself from the bedside. "I got your voice mail, by the way," he'd said. When she'd looked at him, puzzled, he'd added, "The one you left me from Las Vegas. Part of it, anyway. The reception must have been terrible. There was too much static on the line for me to make it out clearly."

She'd remembered. *I just think it's best if I go,* she'd told him, part of a three-step plan she'd pretty much forgotten since then.

"Was there something you needed?" Michel had asked, pausing in Tristan's doorway. He'd given her a pointed glance that had let her know nothing had been wrong with her message to him; he'd received it loud and clear and was offering her the chance to take it back. "Something you'd wanted to say?"

"No." She'd shaken her head. "Never mind. It wasn't important."

Tristan continued that agitated fidgeting after Michel had gone. With his uninjured hand, he pawed weakly at the chest tube leading out from a small incision site between his ribs, beneath his arm, and she caught his fingers to keep him from pulling on it.

"It's all right," she said, trying to soothe him.

"He has to be in terrible pain," Michel had lamented. "The more quickly he heals, the better. It would help him to feed." He'd offered this last with a long, pointed look at her. "Although I suppose I could get a blood bag, hang an NG-feed for him."

She glanced around the room, then leaned over to dig through one of the bedside dresser drawers. When she found a small lancet inside, the kind used when checking blood glucose levels, she pulled it out. Pulling off the plastic cap, she studied the small, squat needle for a moment. Then, without giving herself time for hesitation or reconsideration, she plunged it deep into the pad of her index finger. It hurt, sharp like a bee sting, and when she yanked it back, wincing, she saw a bead of blood, dark and glistening, well up at the point of puncture.

Michel was right—Tristan needed to feed. Even the scent of this tiny droplet was enough to stimulate him, despite his lack of consciousness. He squirmed in bed, tangling his fingers in his sheets, moving his legs restlessly. His eyes still closed, he turned to her, gasping for breath, nearly panting, his face glossed with sweat. Beneath his upper lip, she could already see the telltale swelling as his fangs began to instinctively descend.

"Here," she murmured, pressing her finger lightly to his lips. When he opened his mouth, she slipped her fingertip inside and felt his tongue push against her skin as he struggled to suckle the blood. His teeth descended further, forcing his jaws apart, and his eyes flew open wide, the green-gray irises completely swallowed by his enormous, swollen pupils. His eyes looked like doll's, all glossy and black, and he sat up despite the tangled web of intravenous lines and oxygen tubing draped and arranged around him and the bed.

She didn't know if he was awake or not, not *fully*, anyway, or if he was reacting out of physiological reflex. Clasping her hand between his own, he drew her finger from his lips, then tugged against her, pulling her near. She fell into his shoulder, her head cocked to the side, her throat lay bare and exposed. His breath was hot against her skin, rapid-fire and fluttering, and she felt the prick of his teeth, twin points digging into her skin.

I'm not afraid, she thought, closing her eyes, even though her heart was hammering, and her own breath came in quick, staccato hiccups. *I'm not afraid, not of this, not of Tristan. Not ever.*

There was a moment of pain as he sank his teeth into her flesh, but then the analgesic enzymes in his saliva kicked in, making her numb to anything but pressure as his fangs extended further, delving deeper. When they met their mark, puncturing her carotid artery, he uttered a low, gravelly moan and pressed his mouth fiercely against her skin, forming a tight seal.

She closed her fingers in his hair, suddenly and acutely turned on, not only by the sensation of his lips against her skin, but the soft, muffled sounds as he fed from her. As his rhythmic sucking increased in tempo, so, too, did her arousal grow, and now she was the one squirming, wriggling, panting for breath.

"Please," she whispered, because it was as if he was making love to her, touching her, caressing her, moving her to climax without using his hands, without as much as undressing her. "Tristan, please!"

She came, an orgasm more visceral, explosive, and powerful than she'd ever felt before—without having a finger laid against her or within her. Jerking against him, she tightened her fingers in his hair and cried out his name in breathless release. His mouth slipped away from her neck, and she felt a rush of light-headedness sweep over her from the amount of her blood loss. With a soft moan, she crumpled forward, her cheek settling against the socket of his shoulder. She felt weak, tremulous, and lay beside him. The side of her throat felt slightly damp as the blood flow from her wounds oozed to a stop.

Closing her eyes, she listened to the frantic pounding of his heartbeat as it slowed once more from its own excited, lust-fueled peak. She wanted to raise her head, look up at him, see if he'd lapsed back into the unconsciousness from which he'd only murkily emerged, but felt too exhausted, too frail for even this meager effort.

Instead, she waited. Mason had said that once the Brethren fed from the human to whom he or she was pair-bonded, an infallible mental rapport was born. She waited for this to happen, this uncanny awareness of one another, but nothing seemed to occur. Her perception of him remained—undeniable, inherent, and strong—just as it always had.

"Because it...must not matter," Tristan murmured, his voice coming from fathoms away. His eyes were open now, heavy lidded and somewhat dazed, his pupils constricting back to more normal circumferences.

"The feeding must not matter," he said again. "Because I've always felt bound to you. Right from the start. I think Michel must've been wrong." With a small, crooked smile, he added, "And God, please let me be the one to tell him. Can't wait...to see his face."

She laughed, and reaching up with his good hand, he touched her face, a clumsy caress. "He's my father," he whispered.

She nodded, turning her cheek into his palm. "I know. He told me."

"Davenant said he knew it right away. How could he tell in less than five minutes, and in all of these years, I had no idea? No fucking clue."

He looked stricken, confused, and she kissed his forehead gently. "Don't do that to yourself," she whispered. "You couldn't have known."

"All along, Davenant was after me," Tristan said. "Because he knew. *A brother for a brother, a son for a son,* that's what he kept saying. And Michel knew *that* all along too. That explains him taking my car keys away, his big freak-out the other day." He managed an unhappy laugh. "One of them, anyway."

She moved to kiss his brow again, but he tilted his head, meeting her lips with his own. "Stay with me," he said, pulling lightly against her, trying to get her to lie down in the bed.

"Tristan, no. I don't want to hurt you," she said. He was on the mend, but not even feeding could fix his broken ribs so quickly.

"You won't," he said. When she still hesitated, his brows lifted. "Please. I want you here. I...I need you, Karen."

He looked up at her, vulnerable and pleading, and she relented. Closing her eyes, she settled in beside him, resting her head gently against his chest. "Are you okay?" she asked, with a worried glance up at him.

He'd closed his eyes, resting again, but managed a smile. "At the moment? I'd say I couldn't get much better."

Me, either, she thought as she smiled back. Snuggling more closely, she closed her eyes again, letting his heartbeat lull her to sleep.

ABOUT THE AUTHOR

"Definitely an author to watch." That's how *Romantic Times Book Reviews* magazine describes Sara Reinke. *New York Times* bestselling author Karen Robards calls Reinke "a new paranormal star" and Love Romances and More hails her as "a fresh new voice to a genre that has grown stale." *Dark Thirst* and *Dark Hunger*, the first two books in The Brethren Series™ of vampire romance are available from Kensington/Zebra Books, while the third installment, *Dark Passion*, is available from Double Dragon Publishing. The series continues in 2011 with *Dark Passages* and *Dark Vengeance*, from Bloodhorse Press, and in a free online graphic novel, *Dark Interludes*, available at: www.sarareinke.com.